CAMERONS ON THE HILLS

This is the famous author Jane Duncan's
first book for children to be published
in paperback.

The Camerons, 13-year-old Shona, and her
brothers Neil and Donald, go to their
aunt's house in the Scottish Highlands
to stay. The place is mountainous, often hedged
in with mist, and a marvellous holiday
turns to tragedy with the crash of a
plane nearby.

How the Camerons cope with this disaster
makes a ringing climax to the story.

1971 - 72

JANE DUNCAN

Camerons on the hills

Illustrated by Victor Ambrus

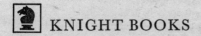 KNIGHT BOOKS

340 03987 6

This edition published 1967 by Knight Books,
the Paperback Division of Brockhampton Press,
Leicester

Printed and bound in Great Britain by
Cox & Wyman Ltd, London, Reading and Fakenham

First published by Macmillan & Co. Ltd 1963
Reprinted 1964, 1965
Copyright © 1963 Jane Duncan

Contents

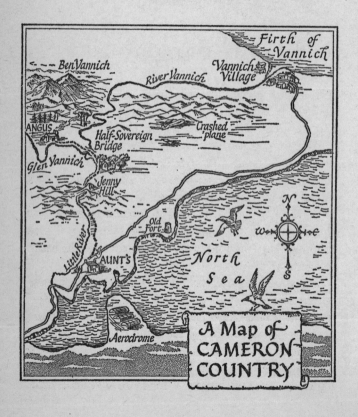

A Map of CAMERON-COUNTRY

1 Hills are dangerous

'No, Neil,' Aunt said. 'It's not a bit of use arguing about it any more. I can't let you go. Ben Vannich is quite a big hill and hills can be dangerous.'

Aunt looked stern and sounded very final and Neil looked sulky and, although he did not say anything more, the very way he breathed sounded sulky too. Donald was neither stern nor final nor sulky but just sat, looking thoughtful, and I wondered if he was thinking the same thing that I was thinking. I was thinking that I had never thought before of hills being dangerous.

There are hills all round two sides of Jennyville where Aunt lives and there is sea all round the other two sides and it is not a bit like where we live at home at Inverdaviot, where we have the doctor's house on one side of us, our garden at the back, and Miss Scott's house on the other side. There are hills round Inverdaviot too, when I think of it, for there are hills at most

7

places in Scotland, but they are not as big as the hills at Aunt's and you never see them because of all the houses, but because Jennyville is only a small village and because Aunt's house is an old farm-house right outside even the village, the hills come right down to her back-garden wall.

Still, I had never thought until this very minute of hills being dangerous. I knew that bulls could be dangerous and might charge at you; I knew, of course, about traffic being dangerous if you did not take care when you crossed the street and I knew that the sea could be dangerous with the tides and the wind and the waves, but I could not see how Ben Vannich which is just a big lump of earth and rocks sticking up behind Aunt's house could be dangerous.

'Aunt,' I said, 'how can hills be dangerous?'

'They've got mist that can come down on you,' Donald said, 'and then you get lost and fall over a pre*ci*pice.'

'*Pre*cipice, Donald,' Aunt said. 'Yes, you are quite right.'

At this time, my brother Neil was eleven and a bit, that made him nearly twelve, and I was thirteen and a half and my brother Donald was only seven and a very small bit and here he was knowing how hills could be dangerous when Neil and I did not know about it. Donald is often like this and although it does not sound very well to say that your brother annoys you, there is no getting away from the fact that Neil and I often find Donald very, very annoying even if he *is* our brother.

I do not mean that we don't like Donald. We like him very much, just as much most of the time as we like our baby brother Iain, but we can't help getting annoyed with him when he is so clever. The thing about him is that he is not like a boy we know called Ronald Smith who is always saying cheeky things and whom Aunt called 'Little Smarty-pants'. Donald is not a smarty-pants. He is just plain clever and knows a tremendous lot of real things. I think it is because he reads so much. Donald is always reading.

'And how did you find out about mist and precipices, Donald?' Aunt asked him now.

'It was in the newspaper,' Donald said. 'About the men that were climbing Ben Nevis and the mist came down and they got lost and one of them got over a pre*ci*pice –'

'*Pre*cipice,' Aunt said.

'Yes, *pre*cipice and when the Mountain Rescue Team got there he had a broken leg and was suffering from *ex*posure. Aunt, what's *ex*posure?'

'Ex*po*sure, Donald,' Aunt said. 'It means that you have been exposed for a long time to the weather – to the rain and the cold – so that the poor man was all chilled and hungry and weak. The word is ex*po*sure.'

I remembered now that I had read about things like this too. I read a book once about people climbing in the Alps and getting lost in the clouds but I had never thought of anything like that happening to Neil or Donald or me, especially on Ben Vannich which you can see all the time from Aunt's house unless there is rain or fog. Somehow, I had never thought of Ben

Vannich being anything like the Alps which are so far away, but now I saw that Ben Vannich was a mountain too, and even if it was not so high as the Alps it còuld have clouds and precipices just as they could. It made me crosser than ever with Donald that he had seen this before I did.

'You and your pre*ci*pices and *ex*posures!' Neil said to Donald in a scornful way and I knew that Neil was just as annoyed with Donald for seeing how Ben Vannich could be dangerous as I was. You see, when Donald reads long words that he has not heard before, he quite often gets the emphasis in the wrong places and sometimes he sounds quite funny but he does not like you to laugh at him.

'Now then,' Aunt said to Neil, 'Donald at least *knows* about the dangers of hills even if he can't quite pronounce them properly,' and after this Neil and I were quite quiet for a while.

Aunt can be a very quietening person sometimes. She is Father's sister and she is much older than Father and she writes books but I think the Camerons must be a quietening sort of family – our name is Cameron – for Father can be very quietening too sometimes, if Neil or Donald or I do what he calls 'going too far'. I simply hate it when Father looks at me and says: 'Now, Shona, that will do. You have gone quite far enough.' And I do not like it when Aunt gets quietening either but she does not do it very often and it does not last for very long.

Neil and Donald and I spend all our holidays with Aunt at Jennyville. When we were younger, Father,

Mother and our little brother Iain used to come too, but now they come only for the long holidays in the summer, and at Christmas and Easter we three travel up to Aunt's by ourselves on the train.

Things often become dull when you become used to them. It is queer, though, that although we are quite used to spending the holidays at Aunt's, it is never dull because it is such an interesting place, with the sea and the beach and the aerodrome just across the Firth and everything and we would be very dis-appointed if we could not get to Aunt's every holidays. That is why we are allowed to travel up by ourselves in the shorter holidays and Mother says it gives her and Father a splendid chance to visit other friends in peace and not surrounded by a horde of Camerons. This is a sort of joke. Neil and I and Donald are the horde because we do not like polite afternoon-tea visiting and get rather bored and people get bored with *us*, I think, when we hang around wearing our best clothes. Nobody seems to get bored with Mother and Father and Iain, though, and Aunt doesn't seem to get bored with us three and we wear old clothes all the time at Aunt's and have fun and everything is all right.

I was now thinking it was a pity that Aunt had had to get quietening with Neil and me on the very first evening of this Easter holidays so I glared across the table at Neil because this idea of going mountaineer-ing up Ben Vannich had been *his* idea in the first place.

Neil is quite different from Donald. I suppose that

is a silly sort of thing to say because everybody is different from everybody else but what I mean is that Neil and Donald are not at all like brothers. Donald is always reading, as I said, and is very quiet most of the time and he has dark hair and dark eyes and wears glasses. Although he is clever about knowing things like how hills are dangerous, he is very stupid in other ways like how he cannot tie his own shoe-laces or buckle his sandals no matter how hard he tries. It is as if his brain cannot send down proper messages to make his fingers tie the knots and fasten the buckles. I suppose his brain is too busy thinking about *precipices* as he calls them.

Neil is just the very opposite. Neil has red hair and blue eyes and does not have glasses and although Neil reads too – we all do, we are a very reading family – he reads in a different way from Donald so that when Neil reads about people doing things, he wants to go and do these things he has read about.

'How did you get the idea of climbing Ben Vannich, Neil?' Aunt asked him, passing the cake to us and not being quietening any more.

'It was a book of Father's I was having a look at,' he said. 'It was about a man from New Zealand and a man from India called a Sherpa who climbed to the top of the highest mountain in the world – Mount Everest.'

'Yes, that's right. It was in 1953,' Aunt said.

'And there was a picture of the two men –'

'Can you remember their names?'

'Sir – the Queen made him Sir for doing it – Sir

13

Edmund Hillary and Sherpa – I can't remember his other name.'

'Sherpa Tensing,' Aunt said.

'Yes and there was a picture of them planting a stick with two flags on it in the snow right at the very top!'

'Yes. What were the flags?'

'The Union Jack, of course!'

'Yes, that was for Sir Edmund but what about Tensing?'

'Oh,' Neil was stuck.

'The Sherpa flag!' I said.

'It was the flag of *Ne*pal,' Donald said. 'Sherpas live in *Ne*pal.'

'Ne*pal*, Donald,' Aunt told him, 'but you are quite right. Sherpa Tensing's flag was the flag of Nepal – What flag did you want to plant on the summit of Ben Vannich, Neil?' she asked then.

'Nothing,' Neil said and looked down at his plate because this was not true for I knew he had packed in his bag, right at the bottom, a piece of string with a Lion Rampant flag and the pennant of his Wolf Cub pack tied to it.

You see, that is the difference between these two brothers of mine. Donald knew all about Sherpa Tensing and the flag of Nepal but Neil wanted to go and actually plant his own flags on the top of Ben Vannich. Donald would never have an idea like that in a million years.

Neil was very quiet now, partly because he had told a fib about not wanting to plant a flag on the top of the Ben and partly because he knew Aunt had guessed that he really *had* had the idea of planting a flag up there, and although I often have arguments with Neil, I do not like to see him all quiet and with a red face like he was now so I said: 'Apart from mist and things, it is miles to the top of Ben Vannich, isn't it, Aunt?'

'Goodness, yes. Miles and miles,' she said. 'I don't know how many because hills are not like flat country. To climb Ben Vannich, I think you have to go away round to the north side and start from there and it is seven and a half miles from here to the bottom of the Ben on this side. I don't think you can climb it from this side – it's just a huge cliff, like the little cliffs on the other side of the Point but much, much bigger.'

When Aunt said this, I did not want to climb Ben Vannich any more although I had been quite enthusiastic at home when Neil first got the idea. The cliffs round the Point were quite high enough to make me feel giddy if I looked down over them and quite grim enough to terrify me if I stood under them and looked up.

'But if you want to go mountaineering,' Aunt said next, 'one fine day, if we get one this holidays, we'll go up to Glen Vannich and call on my friend Angus.'

'Who is Angus?' we all asked at once, because this is a thing about Aunt.

She lives all by herself at this old farm-house but she has a tremendous lot of friends and we have never met one of them who is not interesting. In fact, some of them are downright queer. At least, Neil and Donald and I think they are queer but Father says this is just because they are not like the people we usually meet.

When we are at home, we live at Inverdaviot as I said, and it is a small town and Father is a schoolmaster and Father and Mother have a lot of friends who come to tea or to play bridge or just to talk, people like the doctor and Mr. Ross the chemist and Mr. and Mrs. Halliday who have a grocer's shop and Mr. and Mrs. Ramsay who have the dairy farm just outside the town, but none of them are a bit like these friends of Aunt's. One lot of Aunt's friends come from far away like England or America and write books or paint pictures and there is one that is quite old with white hair who is an actress in London and wears pink velvet trousers all the time. She came for a weekend last year and said she had fallen in love with Neil and kissed him so often that Neil's face was red from Friday till Monday with embarrassment. Then, Aunt has another lot of friends who are the ones who live round Jennyville and they are not so queer as the other lot but they are still different from the people at Inverdaviot.

This is because Inverdaviot is in the Lowlands of Scotland and Jennyville is in the Highlands and the people in the Highlands speak with a different accent and some of them speak a different language even, a language called Gaelic. And when they speak English, quite apart from speaking it with a different accent, they speak it in a different way from us, especially the older people. They never say run-together words like 'don't' and 'can't' as we do; they pronounce all the words completely and properly so that they say 'do not' and 'cannot' and, quite often, where Neil and I would say 'I think', they say 'I am thinking' and in a queer way this makes them sound as if they were better and harder thinkers than we are.

But why Neil and Donald and I find the people round Jennyville so interesting is because they are not doctors or shopkeepers or anything – the only shop in Jennyville is the post office as well and it sells sugar and buckets and sweets and aspirin and knitting wool and everything and it is kept by the postmistress. All the rest of the people are fishermen or shepherds or gamekeepers or things like that and they are all very interesting to talk to and always seem to have plenty of time to stop and have a chat, so this is why we were all interested when Aunt mentioned this Angus.

'Angus is Mr. Angus Mackenzie,' Aunt said.

'Is he a shepherd?' I asked.

I specially wanted him to be a shepherd, for the Easter holidays is the time for the lambs up in the Highlands and I hoped he might let me buy a lamb to take home for a pet.

'Yes, he is a shepherd now – a head shepherd and has two others to help him,' Aunt said, 'but Angus has been a lot of different things in his time.'

'Would he let us buy a pet lamb?' I asked.

'He might, but I'm afraid *I* wouldn't let you,' she said. 'You could never cope with a lamb in your garden at home, Shona.'

'Oh, Aunt! It's a great big garden!'

'But pet lambs grow into great big sheep and it would jump the wall and eat the doctor's cabbages and you'd never be out of trouble. Especially with one of Angus's lambs – they are hill sheep and as wild as mountain goats except with Angus and the other shepherds.'

'What was he as well as being a shepherd?' Neil asked.

'He's been a gamekeeper and a ghillie and a soldier and for a time he was a cattleman on a ranch in South America – a cowboy, you know.'

'A *real* cowboy?'

Neil is mad about cowboys and here is a funny thing. I do not think that until this very moment he thought they were really real. I think he thought they were sort of imaginary people who lived only in the television set and in cowboy magazines. To be quite honest, I had thought that cowboys were imaginary people myself.

'Well, he doesn't have a big hat or six-shooters like a television cowboy,' Aunt said, 'but he did ride a horse and rope cattle and all these things in South America long ago.'

'Will he tell about it?'

'I am sure he will, if you ask him,' Aunt said, 'and if he feels well enough. He came home from hospital only last week.'

'Why was he in hospital?' I asked.

'He fell in his house and sprained his ankle. He lives all alone and might be lying there where he fell even now if the policeman hadn't happened to call at his place that morning. He lives miles away from everybody, you see.'

'What did the policeman go there for, Aunt?' Donald asked.

'He was looking for a stray dog that has been killing lambs, Donald.'

'Had it been killing Angus's lambs?'

'I don't know, but probably it had been. But anyway, you see, Angus is just the sort of person to go to if you want to find out what has been happening away up there in the hills. He lives all alone and that means he has nobody to talk to and look at as we are all talking to one another and looking at one another tonight so he looks at all the things around him and thinks about them. The policeman knew that a stray dog could not have been up there without Angus knowing about it.'

'And had he seen the dog?'

'I'm not sure.'

'And he was lying there with a sprained ankle and couldn't move?' I asked.

'Yes.'

'What did the policeman do?'

'He cycled to the telephone at Vannich Village and then he and the doctor and some of the shepherds carried Angus out from the glen on a stretcher – you cannot get cars and things away into the hills there – and when they got him to the road he went in the doctor's car to the hospital at Rioch.'

'And he is better now?'

'Oh, yes. He wasn't very ill, you know. It was just that he couldn't get around with his ankle and there was nobody to cook his food so he had to go to the hospital for a week. But if there's a fine day we'll all go up and see how he is. Would you like that?'

'Yes, please, Aunt,' I said.

'It is a longish way. We'll have to go right up the valley of the Little River to its source and then over Jenny Hill and down into the valley of the River Vannich. It's about five miles of sheep-track we have to follow. Do you think you'll manage it, Donald? It will be ten miles before you get back home.'

'Of course I'll manage it!' Donald said for he hates anyone to think that he is a baby.

'If we get too tired, we needn't go all the way,' Aunt said.

'Listen!' said Neil. 'What if we see that dog killing lambs? Oh, golly!'

'That is very unlikely,' Aunt said. 'Dogs that worry sheep are very cunning about not letting you see them do it. But we'll keep our eyes open anyway and if we don't see the dog we may see other things. An eagle was seen up Glen Vannich last month. And besides, the walk will be good training for you, Neil, so that you can plant that flag on Ben Vannich later on,' and she smiled at him so that he did not get red or look down at his plate.

'When do you think I could do it, perhaps, Aunt?' he asked.

'In about another ten years or so,' she said.

'Ten *years*?' Neil looked disgusted.

'Yes, if you grow as big and strong as Father or Detective-Inspector Yarde. Hills like Ben Vannich are not places for weaklings, Neil. Men like Sir Edmund Hillary spent years in training before they tackled Mount Everest.'

'What about Sherpa Tensing?' Neil asked. 'He was quite a small-looking man in the pictures in the book.'

'Tensing is a bit like my friend Angus, I should think. Angus is not so very big but he was born in the shadow of Ben Vannich and he knows it and knows how powerful and dangerous it can be, and Tensing was born in the Himalayas and knows about them. Angus and Tensing are both hill men, Neil, and they know about hills. You'd better ask Angus about Ben Vannich.'

'Has Angus been up it then?'

'Yes.'

'Right to the top?'

'Yes, right to the top.'

'Gosh! Did he put a flag on it?'

'I don't know but you could ask him about that too,' Aunt said. 'I say, look at the time! Come along – dish-washing parade, then bath parade and then bed parade for all three of you!'

We helped her to wash the dishes and then we all had baths, Donald going first because he is the youngest. In the holidays at Aunt's, we are allowed to read in bed for a bit before we go to sleep and it is splendid fun because she starts to read or write after we have gone upstairs and she forgets sometimes to come up to see that our lights are out. This first night

of the Easter holidays, though, she did not forget
although I hoped she would because I had a very
interesting book. I had just got to the part where the
aeroplane was coming in to land on the island where the
people were shipwrecked when Aunt came into my
room and said: 'Shona, time's up!' I shut my book
but I could still hear the aeroplane roaring through
the sky.

'Is it a good book?' she asked.

'Yes. I can still hear the aeroplane in it,' I said.

'That's a real aeroplane you hear,' she told me. 'It's
a new flight that comes round by Iceland from
Canada. It comes over here at half past nine on every
Tuesday and Friday evening. Sometimes you can see
it from the bathroom window.'

She went through to the bathroom and I jumped
out of bed and went too. She did not put the light
on but drew back the curtains and there was some
moonlight and a lot of stars in the sky. The bathroom
is at the back of the house so that it looks to the north
and the hills while most of the other windows of the
house look to the south and the sea.

'Oh, there it goes!' Aunt said, pointing. 'See the
little red and green lights travelling along?' I saw them
against the dark sky. 'They look very gay and friendly,
don't they?' Aunt said.

'Yes. Where does it go to?' I asked.

'London, I think. Come along, back to bed! Besides
being friendly, that aeroplane will be very useful twice
a week. It will remind me about lights out for you
people!'

'Oh, blow!' I said and then, at the left-hand side of the window, I suddenly saw something that made me jump with fright. It was like a huge, white skeleton hand, with long bony fingers, reaching down out of the sky.

'Aunt, what's that?' I whispered.

'What, dear?' Aunt asked so calmly that I thought she could not see the thing and that I was imagining it, which made me more scared than ever.

'That!' I drew back from the window and pointed. 'Those big white finger things, Aunt!'

'Oh, that?' Aunt's voice was laughing a little but she put her arm round me and her hand was nice and warm on my shoulder. 'That's Ben Vannich,' she said. 'The moonlight is catching the snow on the summit and lying in the corries of the cliff. Some years the snow never melts out of these corries the whole summer long and this is only Easter.'

'It looks horrid!' I said. 'Like a big clutching hand!'

'Do you think so? In a way, it's rather beautiful, I think, that big mass against the sky, so proud and lonely.'

It did not look so horrid now, I thought, when I could make out the outline of the hill itself as well as the long bony fingers reaching down. Then, as we stood looking at the Ben, a little orange light came on in the blackness away below the long skeleton fingers.

'Oh, look!' Aunt said. 'That's Angus letting his dogs out before he goes to bed. He has just opened his door. Do you see the light?'

'Goodness! Does Angus live away up there?' I asked. 'We can never walk that far!'

'Yes. But it's only five miles. It looks further in the dark. In the morning, if you look out of this window, you'll see the house quite plainly.'

'I don't think I'd like to live away up there,' I said. 'Angus must be terribly lonely.'

'No, I don't think so. He has his wireless set and his dogs and, of course, he has Ben Vannich.'

I thought that Ben Vannich was the thing I should like least of all about living where Angus lived.

'To people like Angus who live in the hills,' Aunt said, 'the hills are like people. He talks about Ben Vannich as if it were a person, a very powerful person like a king. And, of course, it *is* the king of the hills around here – Come along, then, back to bed.'

'How high is Ben Vannich, Aunt?' I asked as I pulled up my eiderdown, for it made it less frightening if you could think of it as something in geography, like Mount Everest being the highest peak in the world.

'About three thousand, four hundred feet,' Aunt said. 'Only about an eighth of the height of Everest, and although it is very beautiful it is very frightening in a way too.'

'Yes,' I said. 'It *is* sort of frightening.'

'But there's nothing to be scared of if you leave it alone and don't monkey with it,' Aunt said. 'To look at, it's all right and quite beautiful. It's only when you try to climb them without knowing enough about them that the hills are dangerous.'

2 Over the hill to Angus

THE next morning, it was grey and cold and the mist was hanging down over the hills at the back of the house like a wet grey blanket and Aunt said at breakfast that we could not possibly go to visit Angus that day, which was very disappointing. 'Anyhow,' she said, 'we have to do some shopping before we go up there, to get something to give to Angus for Easter, so we shall drive into Rioch instead.'

After we had done the breakfast washing-up, Neil, Donald and I held a conference in the boys' bedroom for I had had the idea that we three ought to get a special Easter present from us to be a surprise for Angus.

'If we give one and six each,' I said to the boys,

'that will be four and six. What can we get for four and six?'

'A knife!' Neil said. Neil always thinks that a knife or a pistol is the best present you can give to anybody.

'A book!' Donald said. 'Maybe *two* books for four and six if we buy the paper-back ones.'

I did not think much of this idea either, although it was better than Neil's suggestion about the knife, because we did not know what sort of book Angus would like.

We often buy books for presents for Father but with him it is easy – you just buy the newest book about exploring places like Mount Everest or the Amazon Valley or the newest one about some person in history, for these are the sort of books he likes. And we *always* give Aunt books for presents and she is easier still because you just give her any book at all that has ever been written and she is very pleased. Once, when we were very hard-up, we bought a book for Aunt's birthday for sixpence at the Church Jumble Sale and, to tell the truth, we were a bit ashamed of it although we did not say anything to one another. Apart from being very shabby and tattered, it was very dull-looking and had a Latin name. I looked at that book so much before we parcelled it up and sent it that I still remember its title. It was *Memorabilia Domestica* by a man called Donald Sage.

When Aunt got it, she did not write to us about it as she usually does about our presents – she wrote to Father and he said to us: 'Where did you three get this book that you sent to Aunt for her birthday?'

I felt terribly guilty and ashamed and so did Neil because he got all red in the face and so did Donald because he started to blink behind his glasses.

'What book, Father?' I said although I knew perfectly well he meant that awful tattered old thing we bought for sixpence.

'You see, Father,' Neil said, 'Aunt's birthday comes at a terribly awkward time, so soon after Christmas –'

'– and we didn't have any money, much, Father –' Donald said.

'And it was at the Church Jumble Sale, Father,' I said. 'There was a book called *Blood on my Thumb* for fourpence but we didn't think Aunt would like it and there was this other book for – for – well, it was only sixpence, Father.'

'Can you remember its title?' he asked.

'Yes. *Memorabilia Domestica* – it's Latin but the rest of the book is in English, Father.'

'Well, you bought a terrific bargain,' he said. 'That book has been out of print for years and years and Aunt has wanted it for ages and she's simply delighted. I think she thinks you must have stolen it since she wrote to me about it.'

'Oh, no, Father, we paid sixpence for it,' I told him. 'We meant to save up three shillings to give her toilet soap but by the time her birthday came we had only eightpence.'

'And there was a vase at the Jumble Sale but it was a shilling,' Neil said.

'Well, Aunt would far rather have the book than the soap or the vase. I should always give her books if

27

I were you, and probably Jumble Sale books would
be best but not the Blood-on-my-Thumb sort.'

So, ever since then, we always give Aunt books and
we always buy one for her at the Church Jumble
Sale whether it is at her birthday time or not.

However, I was not very sure that a book would be
the best present for Angus so, when we were in the car
on the way to Rioch, we asked Aunt about it and she
said: 'Four and six – now, just let me think.'

She thought for a long time while she drove the car
over the Little River bridge and on through Jennyville
and along by the shore and then she said: 'Do you
know what I think?'

'No, Aunt,' we all said.

'I think we should all club together and buy Angus
a really good electric torch – a big one like Father's –
and some spare batteries, because he's only got a little
one and its batteries are always wearing out. That's
how he sprained his ankle. There's no electric light
in his house away up there – it's oil lamps he uses –
and he was walking about in the dark because his
torch wasn't working and he slipped and fell.'

We thought the torch was a very good idea.

'How many batteries can we get for four and six,
Aunt?' Donald asked.

'Half a dozen at least,' she said. 'We'll tell Mr.
Macrae that we want a reduced price for buying a big
lot.' She drove on for a bit and then laughed. 'When
we go to Angus,' she said, 'we'll be nothing but a battery of batteries because we have to take up his spare
wireless battery, too, the postmistress told me.'

'His wireless battery?' Neil asked.

'Yes. He's got no electricity in his house, as I said, so his wireless runs off a battery like the one in the car here only a bit smaller. It's very old-fashioned but Angus likes it.'

We had quite a nice time in Rioch and got a beautiful torch for Angus, a long, black rubber-covered one that held a row of three batteries, and Mr. Macrae gave us six spare batteries for our four and six and did them up in a special separate parcel and then Aunt bought a box of sweets and a cake for Angus as well.

When we came home, it was still dampish but the mist had gone away up the hills a bit, and you could see the outline of Ben Vannich now although it had been quite invisible in the morning.

'It's clearing,' Aunt said. 'It may be quite a good day tomorrow.'

We all hoped it would be because now we were all longing to go to see Angus and give him his Easter presents. You know how it is when you have really nice presents for someone which you think he is going to like, you can hardly wait to give them to him. It is just the very opposite from the feeling we had about that dreadful old book from the Jumble Sale that Aunt was so pleased with after all.

When we went to bed that night, I had a look out of the bathroom window and it was very clear and moonlit, with the hills very, very black and the long fingers of snow on Ben Vannich glittering more than ever, and when Aunt came up for lights-out she said there was frost outside.

'What a pest!' she said. 'It will catch that early plum blossom if it gets hard.'

'And what about going to see Angus?' I asked.

'Oh a touch of frost will be fine for that,' she told me. 'It will harden up all the swampy places.'

After she had gone downstairs and before I went to sleep I tried to decide whether I wanted it to be frosty and go to see Angus or whether I wanted it not to be frosty so that we would have early plums in the summer holidays, but I think I must have fallen asleep before I made up my mind.

We three always wake early in the morning, long before Aunt, and I usually go through to the boys' room and get into Donald's bed to keep warm while we have a chat before we get dressed.

'It's frosty,' I told them, 'so we'll be able to go to Angus today because the ground will be good and hard.'

'Hurray!' the boys said.

'But there's a thing,' I went on to tell them. 'Aunt said the frost was all right for going to Angus but it will spoil the plums and we won't have any in the summer holidays. Why is it we can't have both Angus *and* the plums?'

'It's because you can't have your cake and eat it too – sort of,' Neil said.

'Angus isn't cake and neither is plums,' Donald said.

'It doesn't mean cake – not *real* cake, stupid!' Neil told him. 'It's a proverb.'

'You said *cake*, Neil Cameron!'

'I did not!'

'You did!'

'What Neil meant was –' I started to say, when Neil broke in: 'It's as if Angus was a cake and plums was a cake and if you eat the Angus one you can't have the plums one and –'

'I don't want to eat Angus!' Donald shouted and put on his glasses and blinked at us to keep himself from crying.

'What in the world are you squabbling about at this hour of the morning?' Aunt asked, standing in the doorway with her toothbrush in her hand.

'Neil is going to eat Angus,' Donald said in a trembly voice.

'*Eat* him?' Aunt asked.

'I am *not*!' Neil said. 'Donald is just a dopey baby!'

'Am *not*!' Donald yelled.

'Aunt, it was like this –' I said.

'What I said was –' said Neil.

After a lot of explaining, Aunt told us: 'What you are really getting at is that you can't have everything. Nobody ever gets absolutely everything that he wants but today you three are lucky. It's only grey frost and the plum blossom buds will be all right and you can still see Angus if you get up now and dress.'

'And not eat him, Aunt?' Donald smiled.

'Of course not! Anyway, Donald, he's pretty old and would be very stringy and tough,' Aunt said and laughed so that Donald began to laugh too.

After breakfast and that old washing-up that always

had to be done, we packed everything and got ourselves loaded up. Neil and Donald have haversacks. We had a lot to carry, what with the torch, the batteries, the sweets, the cake, the wireless battery and enough food for an elevenses picnic and lunch at Angus's house. Neil was allowed to have the torch parcel in his haversack and Donald had the one with the spare batteries and Aunt had the cake and I had the sweets so that we should all have something to give to Angus when we unpacked. And then we set off.

If you will look at the map that Father drew, you will see how we went.

We left the house by the back door, went across the back garden and then across the road to the path along the side of the Little River, which is really no more than a stream. It is Neil, Donald and I who call it the Little River. Its real name is the Jennyville Burn, so Aunt says.

At the path we turned right and began to walk by the side of the stream and although the map is just a flat sheet of paper, you have to remember that rivers always flow downhill to the sea, so, the very minute we turned to our right we began to climb and the further we went the steeper the climb became. In no time at all, we were all puffing and blowing as we plodded up the path which was of short, springy green grass and very narrow, so that we had to walk in single file and immediately to our right there was high, rough brown heather and on the other side of the stream, to our left, there was the high heather again. There were a few gorse bushes and a few fir trees all

blown lopsided by the wind and it was all very bare and lonely, in spite of the bright frosty sunshine.

'All right,' Aunt said after a little while, 'let's stop and catch our breath and when we start off again, let Donald go in front, Neil. A convoy should always move at the speed of its slowest ship, so H.M.S. Donald will go first and set the pace.'

I looked ahead up the heathery hill in front of us where the stream was coming tumbling down, making a little waterfall here and there at the very steep parts and said: 'How high is this hill, Aunt?' It seemed to me to go right up into the sky.

'This is Jenny Hill,' she said. 'It's about five hundred feet above sea level at the top. But this is the worst part, Shona. When we get to the top, we go down the other side into Glen Vannich, then it's quite flat along the glen for a bit but we have to start to climb again up the valley of the River Vannich to Angus's.'

'Let's get to the top!' Neil said. 'Dash it! I wish I'd brought my flags with me!'

'To plant them on Jenny Hill instead of Ben Vannich?' I asked. 'That's a bit of a come-down!'

'You shut up, Shona Cameron!'

'It's a very sensible come-down,' Aunt said. 'Jenny Hill is quite a good start for any mountaineer.'

'Whee-ee-ee!' Donald said. 'H.M.S. Donald now leaving port!' and he set off up the path and we all fell in behind him.

We had two more rests and I was just beginning to feel that my legs would not climb one more step when

Aunt said: 'Keep going, H.M.S. Donald! You are the best mountaineer of us all. About twenty more steps and you'll be at the top!' and we all began to count.

I had got to twenty-three when Donald stopped dead at a rock in front of him and tried to climb up it by clinging to a little fir tree that grew out of the side of it, so I put my shoulder under his bottom and pushed and he scrambled up.

'Hurray! It's the top!' he shouted and I scrambled up over the rock after him.

While Neil and Aunt climbed up, I looked around and felt rather disappointed at first. I do not know what I expected to find at the top of Jenny Hill but I did not expect to see this big, flat swampy place where there was nothing but a few reeds and rushes and a heap of stones, where Aunt went and sat down.

'Well,' she said, 'here we are. Look at the house down there. It looks like a match-box.'

I looked where she pointed and could hardly believe that the little box was the house where there were four bedrooms and the bathroom and kitchen and sitting-rooms and everything, and that barn outside, which is really very large, looked just like another little box. And then, away beyond the house, you could see the Firth of Arder and the aerodrome on the other side, just as if you were looking down at a huge coloured map, and past the aerodrome a train was going along, looking like a black caterpillar.

Aunt reached into her mackintosh pocket. 'Have

some chocolate,' she said, 'and I brought these. They're not very big but I couldn't carry heavier ones,' and from her other pocket she took out four stones.

'These are for the Cairn, this heap of stones we are sitting on,' she said. 'One for each of us. Whatever you wish is supposed to come true if you put another stone on the Cairn when you reach the top of Jenny Hill,' and she took one of the stones she had brought and put it on the heap where we sat. 'Jenny Hill,' she said, 'I wish for a Happy Easter for everybody!'

Then Neil, Donald and I took a stone each from Aunt and I went first and said: 'Jenny Hill, I wish for a Happy Easter for everybody in the whole world!'

Neil said: 'Jenny Hill, I wish for a thrilling Easter for all the boys in the world!'

And then Donald, looking very solemn, put his stone on and said: 'Jenny Hill, I wish for a happy Easter for everybody, especially Angus.'

I think perhaps that Donald had not quite got over the idea that Neil might eat Angus. Donald often takes jokes too seriously, as if they were real facts that he had read in his newspaper.

'What a lovely day!' Aunt said then and we all turned round and looked the other way, away to the north, and it was like looking at another huge coloured map, but one that was hanging up this time. Pointing to the right, Aunt said: 'Look, that's the Firth of Vannich away over there, another arm of the North Sea like the Firth of Arder, then that's Vannich Village on the coast and the River Vannich. Then if you follow the river inland where it gets smaller and smaller, you come west towards the Ben and that's Angus's house just down below.'

'I see a thing!' I said.

This is a game we play in our family. If you suddenly see something that is interesting or unusual, you call out: 'I see a thing!' and look hard in the direction where you see it and the others have to look and see if they can see what you see. Then you get a score of anything from one mark to ten according to how interesting the thing is. If Aunt or Father or Mother are there, they do the scoring, but if we are by ourselves, I do it.

'What?' they all said and I looked hard, straight ahead to the north down the valley.

'It's only an old church!' Neil said.

'And trees round it!' Donald said.

'Yes, but I still see a thing!'

They went on looking but they did not see what I was seeing.

'You give up?'

'Yes,' they said.

'Aunt,' I said, 'those trees round that church aren't fir trees like all the other trees up here. They look like oaks or elms or beeches. Isn't that a thing?'

'Yes, Shona. That's a very good thing – an eight-mark thing, I should think.'

'Eight marks?' Neil nearly squealed. 'Eight *marks* for some old trees?'

'It's not just the trees, Neil,' Aunt explained. 'It's what they mean and Shona realized that they were

37

unusual enough to mean something. Do you know what they mean, Shona?'

'No. It just seemed queer suddenly seeing that sort of trees – I mean trees that aren't fir trees –'

'Deciduous trees,' Aunt said, 'as opposed to conifers.'

'Yes. It seemed queer to see them away up here.'

'Let's start off down the hill,' Aunt said. 'It's too cold to stay still for very long – The main thing about those trees down there is that they don't belong here. Somebody must have planted them and they are quite big and old, so they must have been planted a long time ago.'

She stopped suddenly beside a spring where the water came bubbling gently up out of the ground.

'This is the source of the Little River,' she said and we all looked down at the little bubbles and the trickle of water that went away past the Cairn and made a little waterfall beside the rock where we had climbed up, a waterfall as small as if the water were being poured out of a jug.

'Is it the rain that makes the Little River so big down at Jennyville?' Donald asked.

'Yes, all the rain that falls on the hillside flows into it and it gets bigger and bigger.'

We walked a little way over the swampy ground among the rushes until suddenly Donald stopped and said: 'I see a thing!' and looked down at his feet and when we all looked it was another spring, the little bubbles sparkling out of the moss.

'Two marks, Donald!' Aunt said and from the way

she said it I knew there was another thing to see but Neil saw it before I did. 'It's the source of another river!' he said. 'Only this one goes –' he looked away down the hill – 'it goes to the Firth of Vannich instead of the Firth of Arder! Is it the source of the Vannich River, Aunt?'

'No, but it is a tributary of the Vannich. The source of the Vannich is away west past Angus's house there at the bottom of the Ben. But Jenny Hill is a watershed. Very good, Neil, you get six marks.'

'Shona got eight for those old trees!'

'I know, but I think the trees are more interesting.'

'Why?'

'Well, we agreed that somebody must have brought those trees here and planted them and that they must have done it a long time ago because they are big and old. Now, why did they do it? It costs money to bring deciduous trees here and plant them. That new little apple tree I planted just before Christmas cost thirty-seven and sixpence.'

'They wanted to shelter their church from the wind and make it look nice,' I said.

'Who?' Aunt asked.

'The people,' Neil said.

'What people?'

We all looked down into the valley ahead of us. There were no people and not a house in sight, unless you counted Angus's house miles and miles away.

'Do you see anything different about this side of the hill from the other side where we came up?' Aunt asked.

39

I had not thought about it until now but this side was very, very different and all three of us spoke at once.

'It's all green grass,' I said.

'And no heather,' Neil said.

'And lots and lots of sheep!' Donald said. 'Thousands of sheep!'

'I wonder if those sheep built that church and planted those valuable deciduous trees round it?' Aunt asked.

We all stopped for a moment and I looked at Neil and he looked at me.

'No!' Donald said. 'It must have been people! It's people that build churches and plant trees – not sheep!'

'Aunt, was there a town here once?' Neil asked.

'Well, not a town exactly, but lots and lots of little farms – crofts, they were called – all over this hillside and down in the glen there by the church and along by the river. It was those crofters who built the church and planted the trees.'

I looked round at the hillside and down into the glen. There was not a person or a house to be seen except our four selves, Vannich Village away in the distance, Angus's house away under the Ben and the ruined church just below us. I looked up at the streaks of snow on Ben Vannich.

'What happened, Aunt? Is Ben Vannich a volcano? Was it like in the Last Days of Pompeii when Vesuvius erupted and buried the town?' I whispered. I felt I could believe anything of that cruel-looking big Ben Vannich.

'No, Shona. It wasn't Ben Vannich that did it. Ben Vannich can be dangerous but it isn't a volcano. No. It was about a hundred and forty years ago that the people who owned this land decided they could make more money out of breeding sheep than the crofters could pay them in rents for their crofts. So they moved all the crofters down to Vannich Village and Jennyville and places like that on the coast and a lot of the crofters had to go away to Canada and Australia too because they could not make a living on the coast. That's why that ruined church is standing there among all those sheep.'

'But where are the houses?' Neil asked.

'They were knocked down or burned down so that the grass could grow for the sheep to eat, but even the harshest people do not like to knock down or burn down a church, so they just left it to fall down by itself.'

'*I* know!' I said. 'It was called the Highland Clearances. We had it in history. But I didn't think of it being – well, like this. I didn't think of nothing left but the ruined church and the big trees.'

'It's churches and trees being where they don't seem to belong and queer things like that that are real history,' Aunt said.

'I know a thing about this!' Neil burst out suddenly. 'It was a programme I heard on the wireless. It was a song.'

'Can you remember any of it?' Aunt asked.

Neil has a terrific memory for poetry and for things that people have said and he often gets into trouble at home for mimicking people too.

'Only the chorus,' he said now, 'because the man sang it three times.'

'How did it go?'

  ' "Oh, Vannich, Ben Vannich, tell us do you grieve
    For the folk of the Glen who now have to leave?
    And borne on the wild wind from some foreign
      shore,
    Will you hear our hearts crying: 'Glen Vannich
      no more'?" '

'Was it *this* Glen Vannich the song meant, Aunt?' Neil asked when he had repeated the verse.

'There is no other Glen Vannich, Neil. Yes. That song was the Lament for Glen Vannich. It was written in Gaelic, originally, in Canada, by one of the crofters who had to leave here.'

I looked away over the empty valley, thinking of the words Neil had spoken, and I felt very sad and when I looked away up to Ben Vannich, I thought of it up there against the sky long ago, just as it was now, while the people went away in a straggling line along the road to Vannich Village in the distance. The Ben must have seen them go and, as the song asked, was it sorry and did it hear their hearts crying on the wind? There was no way of telling. Ben Vannich simply sat there in silence.

'Aunt,' I said, 'Ben Vannich is really like a sort of person, isn't it? I mean, you feel that it *might* remember the people who had to leave.'

'I know what you mean, Shona,' Aunt said. 'Big

hills do take on a sort of personality and in winter when the wind is howling round the house at night, I often think I hear it say the words "Glen Vannich no more"!'

We were now following the river which Neil had discovered and it was growing bigger and bigger and it led us right down to the ruined church in the valley.

'I think we might stop at the church for elevenses,' Aunt said. 'The walls will shelter us from the east wind and it might cheer the ruins up to have people around.'

And so, when we got to it, we went in under the big trees and sat under what was left of the walls. Aunt and I got the biscuits and flask of cocoa out of the haversacks but Neil and Donald had to go and explore, of course, and Aunt told them not to climb about because some of the stones must be loose and might fall, so I went too.

But it was all very dull. It was just four broken-down walls with a broken-down belfry with a lot of ivy growing over it at one end and it was full of thorny bushes and brambles inside.

'Let's go and have some cocoa,' I said and even the boys who are crazy about exploring did not want to look around it any more.

'Would there be any buried treasure in it, Aunt?' Donald asked hopefully when we came back.

'No, I shouldn't think so,' she said. 'The crofters were too poor to have treasure to bury.'

'I see a thing!' Neil said next and we all looked.

'Oh, only half a mark for that!' Aunt said. 'That's

only the skull of a sheep – it probably died in a snow-drift here a winter or two ago.'

When we had finished our elevenses, we put the haversacks on again and followed on down the stream to a place where a bigger stream, which was really the Vannich River, joined our stream and there was a little bridge. We stopped on the bridge to have a rest and we all saw the thing at once but it was Donald who said: 'I see a thing!' and got three marks, for a little way from the bridge, among some rushes, there was a swan sitting on a nest which was built up in the swampy ground like a little island of branches and twigs.

'Let's go down and look!' Neil said.

'Oh, no, you don't!' Aunt told him. 'Not unless you want to have a fight with that fellow along there!' and she pointed further down the river to where a huge swan was coming, hissing and with his wings spread in big angry curves. 'That's that nesting swan's husband,' Aunt said, 'and if you go near that nest he will make you very sorry. Look at him! The Lord High Cocka-lorum of the whole river!'

We threw him some pieces of sandwich and threw some to his wife too but although he ate the sand-wich he did not put his wings down and he went on hissing.

'He isn't very polite,' I said.

'Well, no,' Aunt agreed. 'He doesn't trust us. Be-fore you can get down to being polite to people, you have to trust them.'

After that, we went on without stopping right to

Angus's house but as we climbed up the last little slope towards the wall round the garden, I felt that I had used the very last step that I had in my legs, Donald was dragging his feet and even Neil had stopped talking.

'Well, Neil,' Aunt said, 'would you like to carry on up Ben Vannich? There it is.' She pointed, smiling, at miles and miles of heathery hill going up and turning into sheer black cliff and going up again and turning into white snow. 'Just go right ahead. You can't miss it!'

Neil looked down at the ground and smiled. 'I think I'll wait for a year or two, Aunt,' he said and then she opened the gate and we went into the garden where the crocuses grew on either side of the steep path.

3 Angus catches a criminal

WE were not half-way up the path when the door of the house opened and Angus stood there with a big black-and-white collie dog on either side of him. He was thin and not very tall and had a pointed white beard and he made me think, somehow, of the pictures of gnomes that are in the books I used to read when I was younger. I think this was because there was something mysterious and miraculous about this gay little house with its white walls, bright green door and all the purple and yellow crocuses in its garden, sitting there all alone with that great, towering Ben Vannich sticking up behind it. It was sort of magical, after the lonely glen with nothing but the sheep and the ruined church, that there should be a house here at all, especially a bright, gay house like this with this twinkly, smiling old man living in it.

'So it is yourselves that have come!' he said.

The Highland people often say this when they welcome you, instead of saying 'How d'you do?' or something like that and although it looks queer when you write it down, it is very pleasant when they say it because it sounds as if they are very pleased that it is *you* who have come and not anybody else.

The dogs were a bit frightening, though, because they were so very big and stood beside Angus looking at us so very steadily out of their bright brown eyes. I kept very close to Aunt, thinking of our dog at home which is a little Aberdeen terrier called Whisky and not at all like these two huge creatures.

'How are you, Angus?' Aunt said, shaking hands and then: 'Hello Speed!' and when she said this and bent down a little, one of the big dogs sat down and held up his paw to shake hands. 'Hello, Spark!' she said next and shook hands with the other dog too. 'Angus, these are my brother's children. Shona –'

As I shook hands with Angus, the dog called Speed held up his paw and now he suddenly seemed to be very friendly and not frightening at all.

When we had all shaken hands with everybody, Angus said: 'Now, you boys will go round to the back and lie down!' and I thought he meant that Neil and Donald were to go away and not come into the house at all, until the two dogs trotted off and disappeared round the end of the house.

'What a shame!' Aunt said. 'Sending them off because *we* have come!'

'They will come in later but at first they must be polite and mind their manners,' Angus said and I

47

remembered what Aunt had said about the swan and decided that these dogs must trust Angus.

'Come in now to the fire,' he said. 'It is nearly frozen you must be. There is fresh snow on the Ben this morning and more to come, I am thinking.'

'More snow, Angus?' Aunt said. 'Oh, surely not! When?'

'Oh, not before tomorrow, maybe – you will get home tonight all right – but I am getting the smell of snow in the air today. Now, just sit down and get warm and then we will all have some broth. I have a fine big pot of broth here, just as if I knew I was to have visitors.'

While Aunt asked Angus about his ankle and about being in hospital, Neil, Donald and I sat quite quietly, not saying a word, for we had never seen a house like this before and we were too busy looking at everything. First of all, there was the fire which burned in a fireplace built of rough grey stone. Out of the side of the chimney, there came an iron bar with a hook on the end and from this a big round black pot hung above the flames which rose up from things like enormous dark brown loofahs which, later on, we discovered to be peat blocks, which are really lumps of dried moss and heather roots and things like that. The pot hanging on the hook made Angus seem gypsy-ish as well as gnome-ish, somehow. Then, along one wall, there were three rows of shelves and sitting on them was a whole mass of Willow Pattern china. There were plates and cups and platters and bowls and every sort of dish you could imagine and I thought of the one Willow

Pattern platter that hangs on the sitting-room wall at home and of which Mother is so proud and wondered what she would think of this display of Angus's. Then, up above the shelves, lying across two wooden pegs in the wall, there was a double-barrelled gun and on another part of the wall there was a glass case with a lot of medals with coloured ribbons in it with, underneath it, another glass case that held a very beautiful flag made of velvet, embroidered in gold and with a long gold fringe all round it. The whole room was just as interesting as the museum in Aberdeen where Father takes us sometimes and far, far friendlier, with the bright fire and Angus smiling at us all.

'Please, sir,' Neil said as soon as he could, 'is that a real gun up there?' and he pointed at the wall.

'You will call me Angus, Neil,' the old man said. 'I am always called Angus. Oh, yes, the gun is real enough. Would you care to have a look at it?' and he rose from his chair, took down the gun, handed it to Neil and then sat down again as if nothing had happened.

Neil stood holding the gun in both hands and staring as if he had been bewitched and so he had been, of course. Neil had never even been in the same room as a real gun before and would have been content just to look at it, so that when Angus handed it to him like this it was like some magic that had frozen him stiff as people are in fairy tales.

'You need not be afraid of it,' Angus said. 'It is not loaded. Nobody with any sense keeps a gun loaded.'

'I'm not afraid,' Neil said in a faraway voice and just went on standing there, holding the gun.

'If you like,' Angus told him, 'you could go outside and take a sight along the barrels of it. Rest it on the wall for it will be a little heavy for you.'

'Oh, my gosh!' Neil exploded. 'Come on, Donald! Come on, Shona!'

'Now be careful, Neil!' Aunt said. 'Lay it on the wall carefully and don't bump it or scratch it. That gun is very valuable.'

'Oh, he will take care of it,' Angus said. 'A sensible boy like that will always take care of a good gun.'

Neil was nearly bursting with pride now and as for taking care of the gun, he would not even let Donald or me touch it. He wanted us to stand there and admire him looking along its barrels and through its sights so that in the end we left him sighting up the Glen and went off to explore around the outside of the house.

I had been a bit disappointed when we came through the glen because, although we had seen hundreds of sheep, we had not seen a single lamb, but now, when we went round behind the house, we found a little field with a wall all round it, and inside it was simply crammed with mother sheep and lambs. When we went to the wall to look over at them, Speed and Spark came out of their kennels, which were two barrels lying on their sides by the house, came to the wall and put their forepaws up on it, looking over at the sheep and then at us. Somehow, I suddenly felt afraid of the dogs and then we heard Angus's voice behind us and when we looked round he was at a little back window.

'Look at the lambs,' he said, 'but do not go over the wall or try to touch them. Speed and Spark are guarding them and they would not like you to touch them.'

I stood back from the wall a bit and pulled Donald back too and we looked at the strong black bodies and the big white teeth of Speed and Spark. I did not care to imagine what they would do to us if we did something that they did not like.

'We won't touch your lambs,' I said to them in a rather shaky voice and they jumped down from the wall and wagged their tails, not looking a bit frightening now or as if there could possibly be anything that they would not like.

When we came in to have lunch, it was all more interesting than ever, for Angus took a ladle and gave us all Willow Pattern bowls of broth out of the big gypsy pot that hung over the fire and then Aunt got out our cold meat that we had brought and Angus took the poker and raked a lot of beautiful potatoes, baked in their jackets, out of the ashes. After that, we had a rhubarb tart that Aunt had brought and altogether it was the most wonderful meal I had ever had, I thought, because it was half-way between having a picnic and being asked to lunch with someone who lived in a different world. There was something about the gypsy pot and the Willow Pattern china with all the little men on it going over the bridges with their fishing rods, and sitting by the warm fire while you

remembered that great snow-covered Ben Vannich outside, that made you feel that Angus was a wizard who
might suddenly weave a spell round you.

'Have they caught that sheep-worrying dog yet,
Angus?' Aunt asked.

'No, they have not,' he told us. 'That is why the
lambs and ewes are all round at the back there – that
and my thought that there will be more snow before
the Sabbath. We heard last night that two lambs had
been killed round behind the Ben so I told Kenny and
Roddy to bring our ewes and lambs in close-by. I am
hoping I may tempt that murderer into the range of
that gun of mine,' and he nodded at the gun which was
now standing in a corner by the door.

'You will shoot the dog?' Neil asked.

'Oh, yes. A dog that starts to kill sheep is no better
than a wolf, you know. And once he has started to do
it he will never stop. He was away from this district
for about ten days but he came back yesterday, it
seems.'

'What sort of dog is he, Angus?' I asked.

'I do not know. He will be big, of course, but none
of us have ever seen him. Sheep-killing dogs are very,
very cunning, you see. They are criminals and all
criminals are cunning – it is part of their trade. But
never mind, we will get him yet.'

'Angus,' Neil said next. 'Aunt said you have been to
the very top of Ben Vannich.'

'Oh, yes, but that was a few years ago when I was
a little younger.'

'How many years ago?'

'Fifty or maybe sixty. Since I got a little older I have got a little wiser and I do not try to go away up to the top of the world now as I did when I was young and foolish.'

'Mount Everest is the real top of the world, isn't it?' I asked.

'Yes, that is so, but Ben Vannich is the top of this world around here and quite hard enough to get to. I am quite willing to leave Mount Everest to that gentleman from New Zealand.'

'And Sherpa Tensing from Nepal,' Donald said.

'Yes, we must not forget about the Sherpa for Mount Everest is his own hill after all, like Ben Vannich belongs to the people around here. Sherpa Tensing would be a small, thick-set, strong man, I am thinking, like the Gurkhas I used to know when I was in India.'

'You have been to India, Angus?' Neil asked. 'Aunt said you were a cowboy in South America.'

'Oh, yes, I was in South America – the Argentine, it was – for a while too.'

'But there are no cowboys in India, are there, Angus?' Donald asked.

'No, no. I was a soldier when I was in India. I was a Seaforth Highlander. I was in Egypt and South Africa too with my regiment. I was a piper. That is my pipe-banner on the wall there,' and he pointed to the embroidered flag in the glass case. 'You will have heard about the Pyramids?' he asked. We said we had. 'Well,' he said, 'do you know what we did when we were off duty and went out for a walk? There was a pyramid with every stone about as high as my shoulders and we used to have a race to see who would be first at the top. To tell the truth, it was nearly as hard work as climbing Ben Vannich but of course the pyramid was not as high as the Ben.'

It was very strange to sit at the warm peat fire and listen to Angus tell stories of Africa, the Argentine and India and in the end I decided that he truly was a wizard who could weave spells because he could make the Willow Pattern china and the gypsy pot fade away and you saw instead a sun-baked track winding through a pass in the north-west frontier of India, where a detachment of Seaforth Highlanders marched along, the noise of their tramping boots echoing off the rocky mountains that rose up on either side.

After a while, we all went out of doors again, Aunt and Angus coming too but, of course, Neil asked if he could have the gun again, went off with it, laid it on the wall pointing up the Glen and turned into a Seaforth Highlander on the watch for tribesmen on the north-west frontier of India. It was like Neil reading about Sir Edmund and Tensing – he wanted to *be* them and do the things they did – and now that he had heard about the Seaforth Highlanders on the north-west frontier long ago, he turned into one of them and turned Glen Vannich into the Khyber Pass.

The rest of us went round to the back of the house to look at the lambs again as they all skipped and played in the cold sunlight while their mothers nibbled and crunched at the turnips which we helped

Angus to tip out of buckets over the wall, and then Aunt said: 'Angus has a surprise for you, Donald. You too, Shona'

'Come,' Angus said and led us down to a little building at the bottom of the field where the lambs were. Before he opened the door, he said: 'It was very good of you to come to see me today, especially this little fellow –' and he put his hand on Donald's head – 'for it is a long, long way to walk. But you will get a carry home.'

And then he opened the door and inside there were two fat, dark brown ponies.

'This is Sandy,' Angus said, taking the smaller one by his wiry mane and giving Donald some sugar lumps, 'and Donald will ride on him, and this big fellow is Hamish and you and Neil will ride him turn about, Shona.'

Donald and I fed Sandy and Hamish with the sugar lumps one by one and they were the gentlest ponies, with velvety muzzles, and when the sugar was finished they did not make a fuss for more or turn away scornfully as the swan had done when it had gobbled up the sandwich. Instead, they poked their faces against our chests and made blowing noises in a happy contented way.

'Aren't they polite?' I whispered to Aunt when Angus had gone outside to bring in some hay.

'Yes, just like Angus himself,' Aunt said.

'Does Angus ride the ponies when he is looking after the sheep?' Donald asked.

'No, I don't think so. They are kept to bring down

the dead deer from the hills when they go deer-stalking in the autumn.'

I was thinking that I did not mind going home now that we had the ponies to ride although, before, I had tried not even to think about leaving Angus and his lovely house, when Donald said: 'But Angus, if we take your ponies home, how will they get back?'

Angus stopped with his bundle of hay under his arm and looked down at Donald while Sandy began to nibble one end of the bundle and Hamish the other.

'Oh, that is quite easy. When you get to the top of Jenny Hill,' Angus told us, 'you will just turn Sandy and Hamish round to face back this way and tell them to go home and they will come right back here for their supper.' Then he looked at Hamish. 'You will come home, will you not, lad?' he asked and as if Hamish knew exactly what Angus had said, he nodded his shaggy head up and down, gave a little whinny and then pulled a big mouthful of hay out of the bundle.

'But anyway,' Angus added, 'Kenny will go over a bit of the way with you all for he has to look at the sheep on that side.'

When we left the ponies, Angus showed us a hen with eleven chickens that looked like little balls of yellow wool and then another hen with a flock of ducklings that were even prettier than the chickens, I thought. When I said this, Angus said: 'Yes, but they are a terrible worry to their poor mother hen when they go and swim in the river. She runs up and down on the bank and flaps her wings and nearly breaks her heart.'

'Silly thing!' Donald said.

'Well, I am not sure, now,' Angus said thoughtfully. 'Just think if your baby brother suddenly flew up into a tree. Would your mother not be a little worried?'

Donald's eyes became round like pennies behind his glasses at the thought of Iain suddenly flying up into the sycamore tree at the bottom of our garden.

'It is just like that with the poor hen,' Angus told him. 'She does not swim herself and does not understand how the little ducks can do it.'

When we came back around the house, although we had been gone for quite a long time, Neil was still at his post with his gun pointing up the Glen and, as we watched, he dropped down behind the wall, crawled along and put the gun up in a new place so much as if he were seeing a savage tribesman among the rocks that I could not help looking in the direction the gun was pointing to make sure that there really was not a tribesman there, although I knew that this was Glen Vannich and not the Khyber Pass. It was then that, among the boulders beyond the wall, I saw the thing, just a stealthy, greyish movement and no more, but before I could say anything, Angus whispered: 'Down everybody!' He and Aunt dropped down to their knees on the grass and Donald and I dropped down too just as Speed and Spark came round the corner of the house, but not walking or running. They were slithering along on their bellies like black-and-white snakes; then they would stop dead still for a moment, showing their teeth but making no

58

sound and then they would slither on again. I remember thinking that there was something behind the wall that they did not like.

'Quiet!' Angus whispered and, following him, we all began to crawl across the grass, across the garden path and across more grass to the wall where Neil was. Neil did not even hear us, we were so silent, and Angus reached up very quietly with one hand to Neil's shoulder, the finger of his other hand against his lips, and Neil and the gun sank quietly down on to the ground beside us. It was only when Angus took two bright orange cartridges from his pocket and put them into Neil's hand that I realized that that grey, furtively moving thing that I had seen was the lamb-killing dog and now that I knew it was out there beyond the wall I could hardly breathe. Without making a sound, Angus broke the gun open and slid the cartridges into the barrels and before he closed it again, he took off his tweed hat and stood up a little so that he was looking out between two stones on the top of the wall. Angus's hair was just the same colour as the dark grey stones and, still looking out, he closed the gun across his knees with a very small click which, because we were all so quiet, sounded like a pistol shot.

After that, there was dead silence for what seemed like ages, silence among all of *us*, I mean, for, from behind the house came the baa-baaing of the lambs as they played, got separated from their mothers and then found them again. But the little huddle of all of us crouching with the dogs lying flat round Angus's feet was like a little separate world and I found myself

looking at some lichen on one of the stones of the wall, looking at it so hard that it seemed to turn into a forest where all the trees had green trunks with hard round golden heads, for it was a circle of that lichen that looks like a pincushion stuck full of golden pins. An ant began to walk across it and I was looking so hard that the ant seemed to be an elephant walking through a great forest when suddenly Angus's legs got stiff and straight, there was a frightful bang and then a second one and after this second bang the first one bounced off the cliffs of Ben Vannich and came echoing back to us, closely followed by the echo of the second one. It was very queer, when the noise had died away, to hear Angus's gentle voice say: 'Well, that murderer has killed his last lamb!'

Aunt scrambled to her feet. 'You got him, Angus?'

'Oh, yes, with the first barrel. I gave him the second one just for spite, I am afraid. It is myself that hates a lamb-killer more than anything in the world,' and then he broke the gun open, raised it and looked down the barrels.

After that, he stood looking down at the ground for a moment with the gun hanging over his arm and everything was very quiet and we were very quiet too. I think everybody – even Speed and Spark who sat at his feet looking up at him – was as astonished as I was to hear Angus say that there was something which he hated. Until now, there had been all around him a strange, loving friendliness as when he had told us how the Willow Pattern china had belonged in turn to his dead granny, his dead mother and his dead

61

wife and that was why he took such good care of it; as when the sheep had come to take turnips from his hands; as when the ponies had rubbed against him and had pulled mouthfuls of hay out of the bundle under his arm.

'I think,' he said, still looking at the ground, 'it is because the lambs are so small and full of play and not able to fight for themselves.' Then he looked up, turning to Aunt and me and turning at the same time into a sort of wizard instead of a gentle old man. 'And now,' he said, 'if you two ladies will go into the house and make some pancakes for the tea, we three men will go and bury that criminal out there. I have a fine deep grave dug for him down by the river there.'

'So you have his grave already dug, Angus?' Aunt asked, laughing a little. 'You were sure you would get him then?'

Angus took up the shafts of a wheelbarrow that stood by the garden wall – he used it to carry the body of the dog down to the river, Neil told me afterwards – and he stood there with the great white peak of Ben Vannich behind him, looking more like a wizard than ever.

'I did not *know* that I would get him,' he said, 'but I *hoped* I would get him so I hoped a grave would help things on towards his death so I hoped it in real earnest down by the river there, and there it is, all ready for him, so the three of us will just go now and put him in it and be done with him,' and off he went, trundling the barrow, with Neil and Donald walking behind him.

'Aunt,' I said, when we two were in the house beside the cheerful fire that made the Willow Pattern plates twinkle, 'Aunt, you can't really *hope* a grave, can you?'

'I think you can,' Aunt said, 'especially if you are like Angus. I think you can hope almost anything but Angus is a practical person as well as being a hoper so while he hoped in his mind that the lamb-killer would die, he dug a grave as well as a practical step towards getting rid of him — Well, you and I had better make these pancakes.'

She went off through to a little scullery at the back of the house and came back with a round, flat iron thing with a handle in a semicircle over its top and she hung the handle over the hook above the fire.

'What's that for?' I asked.

'That's a girdle,' she said. 'When it gets hot it is just the same as the hot-plate of the electric cooker and even better because if it gets too hot you can swing it right off the fire. Now, the flour —'

In no time at all, Aunt had made a big bowl of batter with eggs and flour and milk and things and then she rubbed a buttery paper over the hot girdle so that it sizzled and then she started to drop spoonfuls of batter on it.

'Angus can make oatcakes and scones,' she said, 'but he can't make pancakes so I always make some when I come up to see him.'

The boys came rushing into the house and over to me and said: 'Shona! Look!'

They each had an orange-coloured cartridge but

they were only the cases, cylinders of cardboard with
metal at one end.

'These are the cartridges that shot the murderer,'
Neil said. 'Gosh, Shona, he was nasty! Not like a dog
at all – more like a wolf as Angus said –'

'And he had big yellow teeth, all snarling, even
when he was dead!' Donald added.

'I wish it had taken three cartridges to kill him,' I
said. I did not really want one of those cartridge cases
at all but it is a custom in our family that nobody gets
left out.

'Shona,' Aunt said, 'you don't really want a cartridge case, do you?'

'I have a better memento of today for Shona than
that,' Angus said. 'Just you wait till I wash my hands
and you boys come to the scullery and wash yours
too.'

When he came back, he went to a little table in a
corner where a big, leather-covered Bible was lying,
opened it and took out a pressed spray of pure white
heather.

'I found that away up the Glen last summer,' he
told me. 'That is a much better thing for a lady than
an old cartridge case.'

I liked the heather much better and after I had
thanked Angus, he gave me an envelope to keep it
in and I put it carefully into my jacket pocket and
produced Angus's present. Then Aunt and Neil and
Donald got their things for him and when we had
him sitting down at the tea-table, we gave them to
him.

'This is so that you won't fall down and hurt your ankle again, Angus,' Neil said and gave him the parcel with the torch.

'And these are so you won't run short of batteries, Angus,' Donald said after the torch had been unpacked.

'And these are from Aunt and me for you to eat,' I said and gave him the sweets and the cake.

He looked at all the things lying round his plate and then, when he looked up at us, his wrinkly old face looked more like the face of a wizard than ever. He did not say: 'Thank you,' to us; he just looked at us and then he looked down at Speed and Spark who sat on the floor at his feet.

'Did you ever,' he asked them, 'know of a luckier man that I am?' and the dogs swished their plumy tails from side to side over the floor as if to say: 'No! No! No!'

We had all eaten pancakes until we could not eat one more when the dogs raised their heads, then went to the window and put their forepaws up on the sill and a little time afterwards we heard heavy feet come tramping up the garden path. Angus rose from the table and went to the door.

'So it is yourself, Kenny!' we heard him say. 'Come along in now.'

An enormously tall thin man, with bright black eyes and much younger than Angus came through the passage and stood in the doorway, leaning on his tall shepherd's crook with the ram's-horn handle at the top while his two big dogs lay down at his feet.

'Good afternoon, all,' he said to us politely and then to Angus:

'Was I hearing a couple of shots a little time ago?'

'You were that, Kenny,' Angus said. 'Sit down and take some tea but eat that loaf before you start on the pancakes for I do not want you to eat them all. Kenny is the hungriest man in Scotland,' he added to us.

'Did you get him, Angus?' Kenny asked, not seeming to mind the rude things that Angus was saying about him.

'Now, Kenny, would three men like us be wasting good cartridges on missing him when cartridges are such a terrible price?'

Neil and Donald now took their cartridge cases out of their pockets and stood them on end on the table.

'But you had to fire a second shot at him?' Kenny asked.

'No, we didn't!' Neil said. 'We got him with the first barrel –'

'– and the second one was just for spite!' Donald added.

'A little spite in the right place is not a bad thing,' Kenny said taking off his tweed hat and sitting down at the table. 'Well, this is the best day there has been in Glen Vannich for a long time.'

When Kenny had finished eating and he did eat most of the loaf and six pancakes as well, and Angus had shown him his presents, it was time for us to come away and in spite of having the ponies to ride we were sorry to leave.

'But now that you know the way,' Angus said, 'you must come to see me again. And at your next holidays, in the summer, Donald's legs will be a lot longer and stronger.'

'Could we come again *this* holidays, Angus?' Neil asked.

'Surely, if your Aunt says so but only if she says it.' He then looked at Aunt. 'You will remember what I said about the weather,' he told her. 'I am seeing snow in the sky behind the Ben.'

'I'll remember, Angus,' Aunt said.

'Now that that murderer is out of the way, Angus,' Kenny asked, 'will I put the ewes and lambs up the Glen before I go over to the other side?'

'No, Kenny,' Angus told him. 'Leave them where they are for a day or two. The weather can murder the lambs as well as any dog and there is weather in that sky behind Ben Vannich.'

4 Half-magic

ANGUS and Kenny tied our haversacks to the ponies' saddles and while Kenny lifted Donald on to Sandy's back, Neil mounted Hamish and we all set off, Aunt and I walking behind, Kenny in front with the boys. We left Angus at his garden gate and turned eastwards along the side of the river towards the little bridge. When we had gone a little way, I turned round and looked back and Aunt stopped and looked back too. Angus was still standing at the gate but he had turned away from us and was looking up towards the Ben while his dogs lay beside his feet.

The sky had turned to a bright, greenish colour because it was late afternoon and the trees and rocks looked very black and Angus was a small black figure between us and the green sky. He seemed to be the only living thing in that pale green and black land-scape with the great peak of the Ben, its snow greenish white now, rising above it. In a strange way, I felt that the green light was not coming from the sky but that it was radiating from Angus over everything, as if he and Ben Vannich were about to get up to some wizardry or magic.

'Aunt,' I said as we walked on again down the path, 'are there really magic people?'

'Magic people?' she repeated.

'Yes like wizards and magicians.'

'I think *all* people have a little of magic in them,' she said, 'only we all spend so much of our time doing so many ordinary and sometimes nasty un-magic things that the magic in us fades away and dies.'

'Angus is a very magic sort of person,' I said.

'You feel so? Yes, I think you are right, Shona.'

'He isn't magic all the time, though,' I said. 'Some-times the magic is there and sometimes it isn't.'

'Yes. A little bit like Ben Vannich disappearing be-hind the clouds and then suddenly appearing again. When did you think Angus was at his most magic?'

'It was most of all when he said that he had hoped the grave for the dog and then again just before we left the house when he said: "There is weather in that sky behind Ben Vannich." It was as if he had had a private wireless message from Ben Vannich telling him that it was going to send bad weather.'

'Yes, I know what you mean, as if Angus and Ben Vannich spoke a language together which none of the rest of us can ever know.'

'Kenny doesn't believe there is going to be snow, Aunt,' I said. 'Do you believe it?'

'Well —' Aunt hesitated — 'if anyone had asked me about tomorrow's weather, looking at that sky I should have said that it would probably freeze a bit through the night and then start to rain tomorrow but *now* I suppose it will snow.'

'Because of Angus?'

'Yes, just because of Angus — Angus and his communion with the spirit of Ben Vannich,' Aunt said.

'Is there really a spirit in Ben Vannich?'

'For Angus there is because it can make him know things, such as that snow is coming.'

'I don't understand about spirits, Aunt,' I said.

'Neither do I properly,' she told me.

Although Aunt is so old and grown-up — I think she must be quite fifty — she does not mind admitting that there are things she does not understand. It makes her very un-grown-up and friendly.

'But I think,' she went on as she tramped along the path, 'this magic that is in all of us is really our spirit and the more magic or spirit you have in you the more you can recognize the magic or spirit in other people or other things, and the more you can come to know, like Angus knowing that snow is coming when Kenny and all the rest of us have never had the slightest idea of it.'

'I wonder if it really will snow?' I said after a moment.

'We'll listen to the weather forecast when we get home,' Aunt said and then she laughed, 'but no matter what it says I'll be very astonished if we don't have a snowstorm before the weekend.'

'Because of Angus?'

'Yes. Because of Angus.'

When we reached the little bridge, where the swan was still sitting on her nest down below, it was my turn to ride Hamish, so Neil got down but before we went on we sat on the wooden floor of the bridge for a little with our feet dangling over the water.

'I'll give you a hundred million guesses what the name of this bridge is,' Aunt said. 'I meant to tell you about it on the way up but I forgot.'

If Aunt was giving us all those guesses we knew that we would not guess the name in a hundred million years so we all just said: 'We give up. What?'

'Half-Sovereign Bridge,' Aunt said.

If you are anything like me, you probably think this is a very silly name for a bridge. Sovereign Bridge, called after the Queen, would be reasonable, I thought, but half a sovereign was just plain silly.

'Why?' Donald asked.

'It was all because of a plum pudding,' Aunt said.

I began to feel that Angus had magicked us all and that Aunt had turned into the March Hare at the tea-party in *Alice in Wonderland*. I had liked Angus's here-and-gone-and-gone-and-here sort of magic very much until now but I did not like Aunt getting like the March Hare.

'Don't let's talk nonsense!' I said in the severe way that Father says that sometimes.

'It was, honestly,' Aunt said. 'Wasn't it, Kenny? It

was long ago, when Angus was a little boy like Donald.'

Somehow, this was more magic than if Aunt had started off with 'Long, long ago –' or 'Once upon a time –' as the fairy-tales start. Here we were sitting on this little bridge, with our reflections showing in the water down below and the mother swan sitting on her nest while the father swan swam up and down between us and it, looking as if he might turn into a prince at the wink of an eye. Away across the green valley was the ruined church among its trees and behind us I knew there was the secret majesty of Ben Vannich, telling its messages about the weather to the wizard, Angus, while he sat beside the gypsy pot and the Willow Pattern plates. I could not imagine the time when Angus had been a little boy like Donald.

'Angus's grandfather,' Aunt was saying, 'had an uncle who went to London at that time I told you about when the people were cleared away from the valley here to make room for the sheep – at the time of the Highland Clearances, Shona – and this uncle was something like Dick Whittington, Donald. He didn't become Lord Mayor of London, exactly, but he grew very, very rich and every New Year time he used to have his cook make a plum pudding and it was sent up here to Angus's grandfather and granny, but it was no ordinary plum pudding, because it was stuffed full of half-sovereigns as well as currants and raisins and things.'

'What's half-sovereigns?' Donald asked.

'They were coins – I believe the Royal Mint makes

a few of them still but they are not used now – coins about the size of a sixpence but made of gold and they were worth ten shillings.'

'Were there whole sovereigns too?' Neil asked.

'Yes, they were bigger and worth twenty shillings or a pound as we call it. Well, the plum pudding came to the post office in Vannich Village one year and the postman set off up the Glen here to Angus's house, but it was very snowy and slippery and the river was coming down in spate and when the postman came to the bridge here – guess what?'

'He fell in!' Neil said.

'Yes, that's just what he did, poor man, and the river was coming down so fast that although *he* got out safe and sound, his bag with the parcel with the plum pudding was carried away down the river.'

'So Angus's grandfather and granny lost all the half-sovereigns?' I asked.

'Yes.'

'Not *any* of them were ever found, Aunt?' Donald asked.

'Some of them were,' Aunt said. 'When I was a girl like Shona, I spent a lot of time paddling about here – it isn't very deep in the summer, you know – looking for a half-sovereign but I did not ever find one. I know somebody who did, though, and so do you.'

'Angus?' I guessed.

'No.'

'Kenny?' Neil guessed.

'Not me,' Kenny said. 'No such luck!'

'It was Father,' Donald said which made Neil and

me stare at him. 'It is the coin with Queen Victoria's picture on it that hangs on Mother's bracelet.'

'That's right, Donald. Father found it somewhere near the bridge here when he was Neil's age and he was sent up to Angus's with it but Angus's father told him he was to keep it for luck – Look, we'll have to get on. What time is it, Shona?'

'Five past four only,' I said.

'It is time I gathered those sheep in and had a look at them,' Kenny said. 'I will gather them over in the Glen there beside the old church.'

We helped Donald on to Sandy again; I got up on Hamish and we set off across the valley towards the old church among its bare trees. The green colour disappeared from the sky as we came nearer to the church; the hills became grey and cloudy and sullen and suddenly it grew very cold although we had been quite warm while we sat on the bridge. As fat Hamish plodded along, I thought that this change in the weather was something like the sudden changes that had been happening all day, as if we had been moving from one world to another all the time, from the world of everyday to the half-magic world under the Ben where Angus lived among the Willow Pattern china. In the world of everyday, Angus had shot and buried a lamb-killing dog but in the world of half-magic he had hoped a grave for the dog before it was dead. In the world of everyday, Aunt had told us about the plum pudding being lost but when I thought of Father as a little boy finding that gold coin in the river, I knew he must have felt that there was something

magical about it, just as I would have felt if I had found it.

When we came to a flat green place, before we came into the clump of trees round the church, Kenny stopped, leaned on his crook and said quite quietly: 'All right, Glen, all right, Moss,' and the two big black-and-white dogs sped away in opposite directions. One of them went away up the slope of Jenny Hill and the other went up the hill behind the church and after a little time we saw sheep coming from both places and gathering into one big flock on the side of Jenny Hill.

'Moss has missed some,' Kenny said and pointed with his crook to a little hollow in the hillside. 'He is young yet and always in too much of a hurry.'

He then put two fingers in his mouth and gave a sharp, high whistle which made both dogs stand still and the flock of sheep, which had been like a grey cloud moving down the hill, went more and more slowly and then stopped altogether. Kenny now gave another whistle and pointed with his crook and one dog lay down so flat that he disappeared from sight among the quite short grass and the other dog looked where Kenny had pointed, suddenly saw the sheep and was off in a long sweep round the hill hollow to gather them in.

When this little lot had been joined to the main flock, both dogs began to bring them down the hill and now Kenny was making a series of different whistles. We saw the flock of sheep change shape until it was no longer a big, moving, grey circle but a long, grey flowing river in which the sheep were no more than three abreast, and the river began to flow right towards us.

'That is so that Kenny can count them,' Aunt said.

We stood behind Kenny as the dogs brought the sheep past him quite slowly and I was counting too: 'One, four, seven, nine —' when Kenny suddenly reached out with his crook and with its curly ram's-horn handle caught a sheep by the hind leg and pulled it out of the woolly stream. One of the dogs at once rushed up and took charge of it, penning it behind him and separate from the rest and by the time the whole flock had gone past — I had completely lost count of them by now, though — there were five sheep in the little separate group.

'Foot-rot?' Aunt said to Kenny.

'A touch of it,' he said. 'It is the wet weather, I am thinking.'

He took a tin box from his pocket and inside it there was a dark brown ointment. With a quick flick of his crook he plopped one of the five sheep over on its woolly side, knelt down beside it and put some ointment on its feet, then let it go and with a loud 'Baa!' it ran off to join the rest of the big flock. When the other four sheep had had their ointment put on, they ran away too and the flock scattered and began to eat the grass again while the dogs came in behind Kenny and lay down at his feet.

'Which is Moss?' I asked but Kenny did not have to tell me for Moss flapped his great plume of a tail as soon as he heard his name spoken.

'He is not as good at his work yet as his father is,' Kenny said, 'but he will learn.'

'Is Glen his father?'

'Oh, yes, and Angus's second dog Spark is his uncle. Angus's old Speed is his grandfather.'

'It's a dog family!' Donald said. 'Who is his mother?'

'Queen, Roddy's bitch, is his mother,' Kenny told us. 'They are a good strain. It was Angus's father who started to breed them. Well, it is getting very cold but you will be home yet before it is dark. I am going over to the sheep on the other side of the bridge now but when you get to the top of the hill, just send the ponies down. They will go home by themselves as Angus said.'

We said good night to Kenny and came on across the valley into the clump of big trees round the church. It was quite dark in there and the moon was in the eastern sky, misty and silvery and we seemed to have come into the world of half-magic again. It was very quiet, no sound but the plod of the ponies' hooves, none of us saying a word when, suddenly, from among the trees an owl hooted and then Aunt's voice came, speaking in the rhythm of the ponies' steps:

' "Save that from yonder ivy-mantled tow'r
   The moping owl does to the moon complain
   Of such, as wandering near her secret bow'r,
   Molest her ancient solitary reign." '

I knew then that Aunt had felt the half-magic of

78

this place too and that it was that which had made her speak the poem.

'Aunt, are owls witches' birds?' Donald asked, as we came out of the darkness of the trees and began to climb the slope of Jenny Hill, and this made me feel that Donald was thinking of magic too.

'I'm not sure,' Aunt said. 'They say they are. If I were a witch, I think I'd quite like to have an owl about. He is such a nice eerie sort of fellow.'

'If I were a witch – a wizard, I mean,' Neil said, 'you know what?'

'No I don't know what,' Aunt said.

'I'd magic myself a gun like Angus's and go out shooting lamb-killers!'

And now, on the grey hillside, we were out in the world of everyday again and it was not long before we were at the top and could see Aunt's house, away down below, looking like a grey huddle of stone against the darker grey water of the Firth.

'Goodness, it's cold up here!' Aunt said. 'Come along, you two. Jump off and let's send Sandy and Hamish home!'

Donald and I got down and we turned the ponies' heads downhill again as Angus had said.

'All right, Hamish and Sandy,' Aunt said. 'Thank you and go along home now! Go along home!'

'Go home! Good night!' we three said and after looking at us for a moment the ponies nodded their heads and started off down the hill. We watched them go until: 'Look!' Aunt said. 'I bet Angus is trying out his new torch!' and we all looked away over the grey valley to the great white peak of Ben Vannich. Winking round at the bottom of it, there was a tiny little light. You could not distinguish the house or the garden wall or anything. There was nothing but the little light and suddenly it disappeared as will-o'-the-wisps are said to disappear. We were all quiet for a moment until Donald said: 'Aw, he's switched it off!' and, 'He's saving his batteries,' Aunt said. 'Come along, down over the rock and down the path as quickly as we can. It's terribly cold!'

When we reached the back door, Aunt took the key from under the flowerpot where it lives when we are out and put it into the lock. At that moment something fell on the back of her glove and it was a flake of snow. She and I stared at it as if we had never seen a snowflake before while more and more began to fall round us until Aunt said: 'Angus was right, you see, Shona,' and I could only nod my head.

When we were in the house and Aunt was kneeling on the hearth-rug lighting the fire, Neil said: 'Angus said he *smelled* snow. Snow doesn't smell, does it, Aunt?'

'*I* can't smell it,' Aunt said, 'but it seems that Angus can.'

'Like Whisky smelling Father's footsteps on the ground and following him,' Donald said, blinking solemnly through his glasses and making Aunt and me laugh.

'It could be just that, Donald,' Aunt said then. 'Angus and Whisky probably have a keener sense of smell than we have or is it that –' she looked at me and I saw her smiling in the light of the fire – 'Angus got a private message from Ben Vannich, Shona?'

'Maybe,' I said.

'It is *not* that Angus can smell things like a dog or get silly messages from Ben Vannich!' Neil burst out angrily so that his red hair seemed to be standing on end and on fire. 'It's that Angus – Angus –'

When Neil is angry or excited or even terribly certain about something, he can never find the words to tell you what he means, although at other times he is full of words and can remember poems and everything.

'Yes, Neil?' Aunt asked when he had spluttered himself to a full stop.

'It's just that Angus – Angus – is – he is ANGUS!' Neil shouted. 'And don't you dare to say he smells things like a dog, Donald Cameron!'

'All right, Neil,' Aunt said. 'Donald wasn't being nasty about Angus. None of us were.'

'Just you try it!' Neil said glaring at us all. 'Just any of you *try* being nasty about Angus!' and he went marching out of the room, banging the door behind him, and we heard him go clumping upstairs.

As a rule, Aunt gets extremely quietening if any of us get into what she calls 'a paddy of a temper' but although Neil was in a proper paddy now, she did not say a word. She merely shrugged her shoulders and smiled and went off to get the supper.

Donald nearly fell asleep at the table and was allowed to go to bed without having a bath and although Neil was quite out of his paddy by supper-time, he went off to bed at half past seven very happily when Aunt asked him if he would like to go. I helped Aunt to wash up but I kept yawning all the time and as soon as we had finished, I went off to bed too but although I was tired, I did not go to sleep right away. I was wondering what Angus was doing, all alone up there beside Ben Vannich.

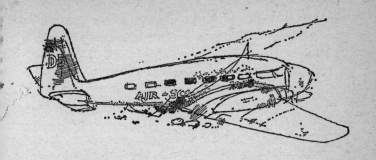

5 We learn to hope

WHEN we got up the next morning, there was no snow but it was grey and drizzly and miserable, the sort of day which is no use for the beach or the hill behind the house or anything.

'Black Friday!' Aunt said, looking out of the back kitchen window while we washed up the breakfast things. 'Look at old Ben Vannich sulking up there with his black cloud blankets pulled up over his head! I'm glad we went to Angus yesterday.'

So was I. Looking upwards to the clouds that covered the hills today, it was difficult to believe that only yesterday we had climbed the hill and walked across the valley in the sunlight.

'Aunt,' I said, 'the weather doesn't change so much or so quickly at home as it does here. At least, it seems not to.'

'It probably doesn't,' she said. 'It's the effect of the hills. You usually get sudden changes where there are hills – that's why I said hills were dangerous, you remember.'

'It is because of air currents and things,' Neil said, 'and warm air going up from the valleys and the winds blowing against the cliffs. We heard about it in Geography once.'

'That's right,' Aunt said.

'You know,' Neil said in a grown-up, patronizing sort of voice while he dried a saucer, 'it was a bit silly of me to think that I could climb Ben Vannich.'

'Oh, I wouldn't say that,' Aunt told him.

'Oh, yes, it was. I just didn't *think*. I knew all about air currents and clouds forming and all that but I didn't think of these things in connection with Ben Vannich.'

'Yes,' Aunt said, 'It is important to connect things up.' She took the saucer that Neil had been rubbing at for about five minutes away from him and gave him another. 'To know about air currents and things and not connect them with Ben Vannich would be like Angus firing at that dog yesterday without putting a cartridge in his gun.'

'Angus wouldn't do a dotty thing like that!' Neil said indignantly.

'No, Angus wouldn't, but *you* didn't put the cartridges of your knowledge of hills into your idea of climbing the Ben, so your idea was just a gun that couldn't possibly fire, you see.'

'Iphm.' Neil put the saucer down on the table and

took another from the draining-board. 'You have to know about more than air currents to climb Ben Vannich,' he said next.

'What else do you have to know?' Aunt asked.

'I don't know yet, but Angus will tell me. I should think that Angus knows about just nearly everything – Look here, what are we going to do today?'

'Well, I'm going to clean up this house a bit,' Aunt said. 'Goodness knows it needs it. It seems to me that this would be a fine morning for you three to write home.'

'Yes,' I said. 'We've got lots to tell.'

'Bags me the killing of the lamb-killer for my letter!' Neil said.

'What are you going to write to Mother and Father about, Donald?' Aunt asked.

'About a Geiger counter,' Donald said in his solemn way.

'A what?'

'A Geiger counter.'

'What for? I mean, why?' Aunt asked, looking down at him.

'If we had one, I think we could get all these half-sovereigns out of the River Vannich,' Donald explained.

Honestly, sometimes these brothers of mine are just about the limit, especially Donald, but Aunt just said, without even a smile: 'Oh, all right. But be sure to explain what you want it for. I am sure Geiger counters cost a lot of money.' Then she said to me: 'Off you go and make a good letter of it, Shona.

Mother has never been up to Angus's and she will be interested in every little thing.'

The boys grew tired of the letter-writing when they had done not quite a page each of very large writing and they began to play Scrabble, but I like to write letters when I am in the mood so I wrote four big pages on both sides, all about everything we had seen the day before, and then it was lunchtime. Then, because it was raining very hard now, Aunt said we might as well drive into Rioch for afternoon tea and go to the grocery for tinned things for her store cupboard which was getting a bit empty. Aunt always has a lot of things in her store cupboard, because in fine weather she often has a lot of unexpected visitors, and in bad weather the roads may be icy or blocked with snow so that she cannot get out to the shops. To live at a lonely place like Aunt's is quite different in all sorts of ways from living in town and goodness knows how different it must be to live away up in the hills, without a car or anything, like Angus and the shepherds.

We did not get home until supper-time because Aunt took us to the museum at Rioch Castle where we saw all the old pistols and swords that were used in the Jacobite Rebellion that ended in 1745 and it was very interesting but not so interesting as Angus's house. When we got back to Jennyville, it was snowing again and very, very cold.

'What weather for your holidays!' Aunt said as we came into the house.

'Oh, we don't mind, Aunt,' I told her. 'Perhaps it will be better tomorrow.'

'And we'll climb up to the top of Jenny Hill,' Neil said. 'We could climb *it*, couldn't we, Aunt?'

'Oh, goodness, yes. You can go all the way to Angus's now on fine days if you promise to be sensible and not fall into the rivers and things.'

'Gosh, of course we'll be sensible,' Neil promised. 'I wish it would be a fine day tomorrow!'

'You'll have to hope for it like Angus,' Aunt said.

'Angus hoped a grave for a bad dog,' Donald said, 'but what do you hope for a fine day, Aunt?'

'Make some preparation for something you will do if it *is* fine,' Aunt told him.

'*I* know!' Neil said and dashed off upstairs so Donald and I followed him.

Out of the very bottom of his bag he took the string with the Lion Rampant flag and the Wolf Cub pennant on it and laid them all spread out on top of the chest of drawers. Then he laid his right hand on top of them and said to us: 'Lay your hands on here!' Donald and I laid our right hands beside his on top of the flags. 'Repeat after me –' he said solemnly like the minister in church, 'I hope these flags –'

'I hope these flags –' Donald and I said.

'– for a fine clear day tomorrow –'

Donald and I repeated it.

'– so that we can plant them –'

'– so that we can plant them –'

'– on the Cairn on Jenny Hill!' Neil ended.

When I went to bed, about an hour later than the boys, I drew the curtains back and looked out of the bathroom window and I looked into what seemed to

be a black wall, with the snow building up on the
bottom frames of the window panes. There was no
moon, no stars, no hills, no Ben Vannich to be seen,
only this black wall with the snowflakes swirling
about in front of it. I remembered how we had hoped
the flags and wondered if we had not done it properly
and then I thought as I got into bed that maybe we
were not such good hopers as Angus. After all, probably we had not had as much practice at hoping as
he had had. Then I began to think of how the
southern tip of Africa is called 'Cape of Good Hope'
and how Mr. and Mrs. Ramsay's dairy farm at home
is called 'Hopeton' and how I had noticed a house in
the outskirts of Rioch as we drove past that had a
plate saying 'Hope Cottage' on its garden gate.

It is a strange thing that if you begin to think about
a word, you find it turning up in all sorts of different
ways and I had never noticed before how often people
use the word 'hope' or how often it occurs in the
names of places and even of people. At my school
there is a girl called Hope Lauder and in our town at
home there is a furniture shop called Hopeman &
Howden.

I thought about this word and how important it
was for so long that I did not open my book until
twenty past nine which meant that I had only ten
minutes of reading time left, but it happened that
this was one of Aunt's nights for forgetting about
lights-out, so I read and read until my eyes would
stay open no longer and I just managed to switch
the light off before I fell asleep.

I did not know what time it was when I put the light out but I seemed to have been asleep for only a few minutes when I heard a knocking down below, then saw the staircase light come on in a streak under my door before I heard Aunt's footsteps going down the stairs. This was something that had never happened before and I sat up in the pitch darkness and the cold, felt for my lamp switch, turned it on and listened.

'Kenny!' I heard Aunt say. 'What's wrong? Is it Angus?'

'No, no, Miss Cameron! Not Angus –'

'Come in! Come in here!' Aunt said in a hurried voice. 'There's an electric fire in here.'

I heard them go into the big sitting-room which Aunt does not use except when she has a lot of grown-up visitors and I heard the door shut. Somehow, then, I began to feel scared. It was so terribly cold and there were frost ferns on my window-panes now and it was so creepy with just a low murmur of voices coming up from the room below. I crept out of bed, put on my slippers and tiptoed along to the boys' bedroom but they were both fast asleep – I could hear them breathing in the darkness – and I was afraid of waking them yet I felt I just had to, so as not to be alone like this.

'All right, Shona, come down,' I heard Aunt's voice say quietly from the bottom of the stairs.

Thankful and shivering, I ran down as quietly as I could.

'The boys aren't awake?' she asked. I shook my

head. 'And you've no dressing-gown. Never mind. Look, put your coat on.'

She took my coat from its hook in the hall and helped me into it. 'Come in to the fire,' she said.

Kenny was sitting there, his two dogs at his feet, his tall crook held upright in his hand so that the curly ram's horn of its handle cast a huge shadow on the wall, and his face looked sad and solemn.

'A dreadful thing has happened, Shona,' Aunt said. 'The Friday night aeroplane has crashed up behind Jenny Hill.'

I thought of that green valley we had crossed on the way to Angus; I thought of the ruined church and the loneliness of it all and how, now, it must be black dark and covered with snow and terrible. I felt as if my heart was swelling up inside me until it would burst.

'You and I have to try to help, Shona.'

'How?' I managed to say.

'We must light fires and get lots of hot water. When – if – when they find the people, they are going to bring them down over Jenny Hill.'

I thought of all that heather and swamp land which was now covered with snow.

'But how?' I asked.

'If they cannot walk, we will carry them,' Kenny said.

'There is no hope of getting transport in from the Vannich end?' Aunt asked.

Kenny shook his head. 'The doctor's car is stuck in a snowdrift about three miles in. The snow is far deeper up there than on this side.'

He stood up and laid aside the glass he had been drinking from.

'All right, Kenny,' Aunt said. 'We'll get everything ready and if there's anything else we can do, get a message down to me.'

'I will do that,' Kenny said and his Highland way of saying it made it sound like a true promise. 'I will be going back up there now.'

'Shona, go and put on your trousers and your warmest sweater,' Aunt said, 'and try not to wake the boys.'

When I went upstairs, I looked at my watch and it was twenty to four in the morning. While I was putting on my clothes, I had a feeling that I must be dreaming but when I came downstairs I saw a little heap of frozen snow on the hall floor and I knew that it must have dropped from Kenny's boots.

It was so terribly cold at first that my teeth chattered and my brain would not work so I do not remember the first part clearly, but I remember Aunt giving me a cup of cocoa and a biscuit and then I felt better.

'Now,' she said, 'do you think you can creep up and down the stairs without waking the boys and bring down all the blankets from your room and mine and all the spare ones out of the chest in the cupboard?'

It was less creepy now that I had something to do and while I tiptoed up and down, up and down, Aunt lit fires in the big sitting-room, our little living-room that we use all the time and the big dining-room that is hardly ever used at all. Then she lit the old donkey boiler in the kitchen which had not been used since she installed electricity in the house and she boiled kettles and filled all the hot-water bottles.

'Aunt, how many people are there?' I asked while she laid out on the table all the cans of soup we had bought in Rioch that very day or, rather, the day before, for it was Saturday morning now.

'We don't know,' she told me.

'Who will bring them down? Kenny and Angus?'

'Oh, there are lots of people up there helping. The doctor and the police from Vannich are there and there's a Mountain Rescue team coming over from the aerodrome. Hush! What's that?'

We went to the front door and saw three ambulances and a car pulling up at the gate.

'Miss Cameron?' a man's voice asked.

'That's right.'

'I am Doctor Renfrew from the hospital,' the voice said. 'We were told to report here.'

'Yes, Doctor. You had better come in,' Aunt told him.

'We haven't – that is, nobody has come down from the hills yet.'

The doctor and six men in uniform came trooping into the house and Aunt asked me to make a big pot of tea while they all asked her questions.

'I don't know,' she kept saying, 'I just don't know. I've seen nobody but one of the hill shepherds who came down with a message from the Vannich doctor up there.'

While I waited for the kettle to boil, I pulled back the curtains and looked out of the scullery windows and it was no longer like a black wall outside. The snow had stopped falling, the air was clear, the sky sparkling with stars and away in the distance Ben Vannich was glittering all over with snow while the long streamers of the Northern Lights sprang up into the sky behind it. Between the Ben and the top of Jenny Hill behind the house, the slopes were alive with moving lights as if dozens of big glow-worms were moving about up there and I suddenly realized that these lights were the men who were looking for the people from the aeroplane.

The kettle boiled, I made the tea and carried the tray through to Aunt and the men and then I went back to the window and went on looking up the hill. I suddenly remembered the word 'exposure' which Donald had pronounced '*ex*posure' and thought of all those people lying injured and helpless in the frosty snow.

'I hope – I hope –' I began to say to myself and I wanted to cry because I did not really know how to hope to make the thing come true and I could only go on saying 'I hope – I hope –' in my mind and I could not stop.

Then my eyes began really to see again and I saw a light coming bob-bobbing down Jenny Hill and then it came across the road to our back gate and the light was a lantern tied to a stretcher which two men were carrying between them. I felt like screaming but Aunt does not like people to scream so I swallowed hard, went to the door of the living-room and said, as quietly as I could, so that it was just a whisper that came out: 'Aunt, two men are coming with a stretcher.'

Aunt stood up and looked at me and I saw her throat move as she swallowed hard just as I had done. She and the doctor and two of the ambulance men came to the kitchen and opened the door, and a police-man came in first, then the stretcher and then another man. I was afraid even to look at the stretcher until I heard a lady's voice say: 'Hello, little girl,' and then I saw a white-haired old lady lying there and she was even smiling a little.

The policeman handed a piece of paper to the doctor, who looked at it and then said: 'Some hot tea, Miss Cameron, please,' and then he said to the men with the stretcher: 'Take her through to the fire.'

'Shona,' Aunt said to me, 'get the tea for the lady. I see another stretcher coming down.'

It went on like that for hours. Daylight broke and still the stretchers kept on coming down over the frozen hill and I went on pouring cups of tea, making more tea, emptying hot-water bottles and refilling them while the stretchers passed through the kitchen and on into the downstairs rooms where the fires were, while the ambulances drove away and more ambu-lances kept coming.

'Shona,' Aunt said at one point when it was day-light, 'the boys are awake. Go up and get them dressed for out of doors and get them to spread kitchen salt on the door-step and wherever it is needed. When

the salt is finished, tell them to get cinders from the ash-pit and spread those.'

The boys really did awfully well and I was proud of them. The coarse salt was finished in no time and slippery patches kept developing everywhere and Neil and Donald shovelled cinders from the ash-pit into buckets, carried them round to the road and spread them under the wheels of the ambulances so that the tyres could take a grip as they moved off. The boys did not even say they were hungry, although Neil is something like Kenny and gets hungry all the time, until I suddenly remembered that they had had no breakfast and ran out to them with big thick slices of toast and just at that moment I discovered that I was using the last packet of tea in the kitchen and had to send them careering off to the village shop.

By this time, there was a huge crowd of people out on the road around the house – I did not know there were so many people in the whole Jennyville district – and a woman heard me sending the boys for tea and she and some of the others went away and came back with all the tea and milk and sugar that they had in their own houses. Aunt asked two of them to come in and help me in the kitchen so it was not such a rush after that.

It is quite impossible to tell about it all, though. When a dreadful thing happens, like that aeroplane crashing, it seems to me that you start to live in a different world where different things become important. It seems queer to say that when all these stretchers were coming into the house, right past me, I hardly

looked at them because the only thing that was important to me was to keep the kettles boiling, keep up the supply of hot tea for the injured people and the helpers and fill hot-water bottles when they were handed to me, but that is how it was. It was as if there was nothing in the world except these jobs that Aunt had told me to do and I simply had to keep on doing them.

Quite suddenly, I came back out of this strange different world into the real world of everyday. Mrs. Bain and Mrs. Macintyre, the two neighbours from the village who had been helping me, wiped off the draining-board at the sink and hung all the wet dish-towels above the stove and then Mrs. Bain said: 'Just tell your Auntie that we've gone home, Shona, but if she wants us to help her to clean up the house or anything, she is just to send Neil down for us.'

'Have all the people been found?' I asked.

'Yes. So the policeman says.'

I suddenly thought about all these stretchers that had come through the kitchen – really thought about them – and connected up in my mind what they meant.

'Are they all – all right, Mrs. Bain?' I asked.

'Yes. The whole thirty-seven of them,' she said. 'Most of them are not even badly hurt so don't you worry about them, pet. They are all nice and warm in the hospital now. The poor pilot of the aeroplane is the worst – he has a broken leg and a broken arm but he will be all right the doctor says. Now, don't you cry, Shona. They will all be all right.'

But I could not stop crying so I ran away out through the back door and round to the barn and let Mrs. Bain and Mrs. Macintyre go home to the village. I sat in Aunt's car in the barn and cried for a long time but I was really crying because the hope I had hoped about the people in the aeroplane had come true and none of them had been killed.

'Shona! Shona!' I heard Neil and Donald calling after a long time.

I mopped up my face with the duster that Aunt keeps in the car and grabbed the big yard broom that stands in a corner of the barn. When you are the oldest one of a family like I am, you feel you have to behave as if you were even older than you are. It was all right for Neil and Donald to be shouting round the garden after me in worried voices because they could not find me now that all the excitement was over but it would never do for me to go shouting in a worried voice for Aunt, although that is what I felt like doing. Neil and Donald had come back from a world full of carrying cinders, I knew, just as I had come back from a world of nothing but boiling kettles, into the real world of everyday, and I was part of their real world and they were worried because they could not find me and when I did go out of the barn I had to be my everyday self that they knew and not somebody all splooshy with crying because my hope that I had hoped had come true.

But I did not really feel like my everyday self after everything that had happened. Neil and Donald were quite 'everyday' now and I discovered that this was because they were not quite old enough to connect up everything in their minds about how the people might all have been killed when the aeroplane crashed. For them, it had been a change from everyday things to carry cinders and help the ambulance men and all quite exciting and not sad or dreadful or anything. Until now, I had always felt a bit boasty inside myself about being the eldest of the family but I knew now that I had never really *felt* the eldest. I had been like Neil and Donald but now I was not quite like them any more. I was older; I was older in my mind and I had done much more connecting up about the aeroplane crashing than they had and that was why it was difficult for me to get back to being my everyday self that they knew. I decided that the best thing to do was to be what they call 'uppitty and bossy' and then they might not notice that I had been crying.

'Neil,' I said, coming out of the barn, 'take this broom and sweep all those big cinders off the back yard before any more of them get carried into the house! Donald, get the kitchen broom and help Neil!'

'I'm fed up to my back teeth with cinders!' Neil said but he took the broom and we cleaned up the yard a bit and then put some finer cinders back on the frozen steps and made a little cinder path to the coal-cellar.

'I'm so hungry,' Neil said, 'that the front of my stomach is sticking to the back.'

'Mine too,' Donald said.

'All right,' I told them. 'You finish off this path while I go in and see Aunt.'

The house was very quiet and it looked like the beach does after a stormy night when the big waves have been pounding in, leaving great heaps of seaweed and driftwood behind. In the living-room, there were blankets and eiderdowns in heaps everywhere, empty tea-cups and glasses sitting about, hot-water bottles that had gone cold drooping over the edge of the sofa in the dreary way that cold hot-water bottles do and the fire was very nearly out. I put some coal on it and then I heard voices through in the big sitting-room so I went through there.

It looked very much like the living-room, only worse, because there had been more people in it, and Aunt, the doctor from Vannich and another man were there. It was astonishing, somehow, to discover that this other man was Angus. I had never thought of him being here in Aunt's house. In my mind he belonged in his own lovely house, by his fire with the gypsy pot and the Willow Pattern china or in his garden with Ben Vannich towering up behind him.

'Here is a girl who did well this terrible night and morning,' he said when I went into the room.

I am telling about this because Angus saying that made me feel prouder than I have ever felt in my life. I read a book once and the hero was a young soldier who was killed at the Battle of Waterloo and buried on the battlefield, but his father and mother, on the family gravestone in their English village churchyard, got the mason to carve: 'In memory of Thomas who did well at Waterloo.' So, when Angus said what he did, I felt as proud as if I had been to Buckingham

Palace and had got a medal from the Queen because I knew, somehow, that you had to do really well before Angus would say it.

'I must go and see about some lunch,' Aunt said as soon as I went in and she went away to the kitchen so I stayed with Angus and the doctor for a little while.

'Angus,' I asked, 'who found out that the aeroplane had crashed away up there?'

'It was Angus himself,' the doctor told me.

I stared at Angus, wondering about it all, for he has no telephone and no car up at his house and, as if he knew what I was thinking, he said: 'I look forward to the aeroplanes coming over on Tuesday and Friday evenings. When you live in a lonely place like me, you look forward to all kinds of different things and when half past nine came and I did not hear the aeroplane, I began to wonder about it for it is always as regular as a clock. And then, the weather was bad, very bad, up there and I got worried and in the end of it I did not go to bed. It was after one in the morning before the aeroplane came and as soon as I heard it I knew that something was wrong for it was not making its usual sort of noise and then, before I could get my coat on and get outside, there was a terrible loud bang and I thought the aeroplane had hit the cliffs of the Ben. When I went out, it was flying very low over the Glen and red flames were pouring out of one side of it so I ran into the house and got my torch that you gave me and my gun and my bag of cartridges. Down at my garden gate, I loaded the gun and fired two shots and then I ran away across the Glen after the aeroplane but every now and again I stopped and fired off another two shots. By this time I could see the aeroplane lying on the side of the hill behind the church, and I knew that the shots would bring Kenny and Roddy for they know that I am not one to be wasting cartridges in the middle of the night for no reason when they are such a price. So that is how it was that we all got to the aeroplane, Shona.' Angus now turned to the doctor. 'I had no idea, Doctor,' he said, 'that those flying machines were so big.'

I remembered that the first time I had been close to a big aeroplane I had not even *recognized* it because it was so big and I was looking about underneath its wings for the aeroplane that I had come to see.

'Is the aeroplane all burned away?' I asked.

'No,' the doctor told me. 'It was one engine that went on fire but that engine fell off before the aeroplane crashed which was a mercy. The burned-out engine and one wing are lying a good two miles away from the rest of the aeroplane – that was why the people were so scattered.'

'They all fell out?' I asked.

'Most of them did and the ones who fell out are not so badly hurt as the pilot and the ones who were still inside. The soft, deep snow helped them a bit, you see.'

Aunt came then and told us to come for lunch which was soup and bully beef and potatoes and a milk pudding which is very dull as a lunch but I was so hungry that I could have eaten the hard tack and Yankee leather that Father talks about sometimes.

I felt, now that we had got all the people down off the hill and safely away to the hopsital, that we should all be very happy but, somehow, Aunt and the doctor and Angus were not really happy and when Neil asked Aunt over the lunch table if we could go up and see the crashed aeroplane, she said very sternly: 'Eat up your potatoes, Neil, and don't talk any more about the aeroplane now, please.'

This was not a bit like Aunt as she usually is and it made me look at her really hard. It was then that I noticed that her face was different in a queer way and it took me a long time to discover that she had been crying for I had never even thought before of Aunt crying and I could hardly believe now that she *had* been. To tell the truth, I did not *want* to believe it because it was too frightening, in the same queer way that Ben Vannich had been frightening that first night I saw the skeleton fingers of snow reaching up into the sky.

Neil and Donald and I did not talk any more at the lunch table and when the meal was finished Aunt did not ask us to help with the washing-up as she usually does. I thought this might be because the doctor and Angus were with us so I asked her if the boys and I should wash up while she sat down in the other room.

'Oh, don't bother with the dishes, Shona,' she said. 'Aren't you and the boys tired? Wouldn't you like to go up to the boys' room and read for a while?'

'We'd rather go out,' I said. 'It's a lovely day.'

'Oh, very well then. Off you go but wrap up well and put on your Wellington boots.'

I did not really want to go out at all. I was too worried about Aunt.

'Something's the matter with Aunt,' I told the boys when we were all outside the back door.

'Is she feeling sick?' Donald asked.

'Has she got a headache?' Neil asked.

'I don't know!' I said crossly. I always get cross when the boys ask me questions and I do not know the answers. 'Anyway,' I told them, 'I'm not leaving this house and Aunt to go anywhere this afternoon, so there!'

'Then we might as well wash all those old dishes,' Neil said grumpily. 'There's nothing else to do.'

We came back into the kitchen and took off our coats and things and started to do the dishes but I was all in a muddle inside my head. It was only a little after twelve noon and I had been up for so long that I felt it should be twelve midnight instead of bright daylight with the sun sparkling on the frozen snow, yet I did not feel tired or sleepy or that I wanted to go to bed. I simply felt all in a muddle inside myself, as I said.

We were putting the last of the clean dishes away in the cupboard when Kenny and another man came clumping across the yard to the back door but before we could even open it, Aunt was there saying: 'Kenny! You've found – anything?'

I knew before she finished speaking that Kenny had not found whatever she wanted him to have found and so did she – you could tell it from how her voice trailed away into nothing – and there was no need for Kenny to shake his head from side to side the way he did.

'Will you telephone to the hospital?' Kenny asked. 'We promised to telephone to them about twelve.'

'Yes,' Aunt said in a tired voice. 'The doctor is still here. He will do it. But you are still searching?'

'Oh, yes. There are over a hundred men on the Ben and more coming.'

I gave the sleeve of Neil's sweater a tug; he gave Donald's sleeve a tug and the three of us ran away upstairs. Aunt has two telephones – one downstairs and one upstairs beside her bed – and I went into her bedroom and lifted the receiver in there.

'Shona!' Neil said in a horrified whisper.

'Oh, *Shona!*' Donald said in a deep husky voice and blinked hard behind his glasses.

'Shut up!' I said to them and then they crowded in round the receiver.

It was a little time before the click came as the doctor lifted the downstairs telephone and we heard the dial spinning, then the telephone ringing in the hospital.

'Doctor Renfrew, please,' he said then.

'Renfrew here,' the voice said.

'We've just had a message from the hills –'

'They've got the baby? Is he –'

'No, Renfrew. There are over a hundred men and forty sheep dogs on the Ben and they haven't found a trace of the child.'

'Oh –'

The doctors went on talking to one another but I put the receiver back on the rest, not caring whether they heard the click it made or not and then I began to cry, sitting on Aunt's bed. I simply could not help it. It was so terrible to think of that poor baby lying somewhere in the snow on that dreadful Ben Vannich that I simply could not help it.

'Shona, don't cry,' Neil said.

'No, don't cry, Shona,' Donald said and his voice was all trembly.

'It's because of the baby,' I said. 'You heard about the baby?'

The boys nodded.

'Oh, if only we could *do* something!' I said. 'It's because of not being able to do anything that I am crying.'

We were all quiet for a little while till Donald said in a soft little voice: 'Shona, could we *hope* something, maybe?'

Hoping did not seem to me to be much use with all these men and dogs searching all this time but it was something to do.

'What can we hope?' I asked, trying to stop crying.

'*I* know!' Neil said and went off to the boys' room so Donald and I followed him.

Out of a drawer, Neil took the cartridge case that Angus had given him the day before and I knew that he was bringing out the thing he treasured most. He put it on the chest of drawers where his flags were still lying.

'I hope this,' he said.

Donald now took his cartridge case from another drawer and put it beside Neil's.

'And I hope mine,' he said.

Then I went away to my room, took my envelope with the spray of white heather out of the drawer, went back to the boys and put it beside the cartridge cases.

'I hope this,' I said.

'Put your hands beside the things and repeat after me —' Neil said. 'We hope these three things and will give them to the baby when he is found.'

In a queer way, I felt better after we had said it and I was not crying any more.

'It worked with the flags, after all,' Neil said after a moment.

'This *is* a fine day and we could have planted the flags on Jenny Hill if it hadn't been — been for the aeroplane.'

'And carrying cinders and things, Shona,' Donald added.

'Yes,' I said. 'That's true,' but I still wished there was something more we could do.

'Shona! Neil! Donald!' Aunt's voice called. 'Are you upstairs?'

'Yes, Aunt,' we called back and ran to the landing.

'Come down and help me! We've got the ponies outside and we are going to take food up to the men on the hills!'

We ran helter-skelter downstairs. It was so splendid to feel that there was something we could really do.

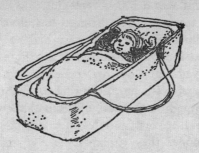

6 A hope comes true

DOWNSTAIRS, the kitchen was like the canteen kitchen at Father's school, with great thermos buckets full of soup and stew that had been sent out from Rioch, and in the back yard there were not only Hamish and Sandy but six more ponies as well, all tossing their manes and blowing steam into the frosty air. Instead of saddles, they all had big baskets hung from straps across their backs and Angus and some other men were loading the thermos buckets into the baskets, along with bowls and bread and bundles of spoons. When everything was ready, Aunt said: 'I'll just get my coat,' and Angus said: 'But there is no need for *you* to go up there, Miss Cameron!'

'I'm going!' Aunt said, glaring round at everybody. 'I can't sit in this house one more minute, Angus! You'll just stay here with the doctor and keep the fire going. I'm going up there!'

I had never seen Aunt look like this or speak like

this before. It was a little frightening and yet it was comforting too because she seemed to feel very much as I had felt upstairs just after we had hoped, as if her feet and legs were itching so that she could not keep still. Neil and Donald stood gaping at her and I knew they were feeling just as I felt when Aunt went whirling through to the hall and came back with her mackintosh, her scarf and her heavy brogue shoes. And no wonder they gaped, for she glared out of the window at Ben Vannich as if she intended to go up there, pull it to pieces and throw it all into the sea.

'Go and get your coats on!' she snapped at us as she stamped into her heavy shoes. 'Don't stand there gaping as if there was nothing to be done! And put on your heavy shoes – you can't get a foothold on the hills today in these rubber boots. If your feet get wet it doesn't matter for once!'

We ran off and scrambled into our things, then rushed back to the kitchen and the whole procession of us started off up Jenny Hill.

It was not easy to climb the steep slope over the frozen snow but we found that here and there stout posts had been driven into the ground at the most slippery places so that you could catch hold and pull yourself up by them. The ponies seemed to find it much easier than we did but Aunt said that that was because they were hill ponies, born among the hills, and they had a special instinct for finding the best places for gaining a foothold.

When we came to the little rock at the top where

we had to climb up, the ponies went off round in a semicircle by themselves and came back to join us on the flat place on the summit. Then we started to go down into the valley which was much easier.

'Look!' Neil shouted suddenly. 'I see the aeroplane!' and, looking where he pointed, we could see the aeroplane with only one wing, all glittering in the sun, lying on the side of a hill away beyond the old church. I looked up at Aunt, saw her staring at the wreckage which, from here, looked like one of Donald's toy aeroplanes that had got broken and then Aunt looked away west to the Ben. Ben Vannich, even from here, did not look like a toy. It was standing up against the sky, massive and proud and glittering and somehow I felt that it too could see the broken aeroplane but that it did not care, because it was so old and had seen so many things and that, from its great height, the aeroplane was just no more than a crumpled leaf that had fallen to the ground.

'You see where the other wing is lying?' one of the men said to Aunt and pointed towards the bridge where we could see it quite clearly, lying on a black patch among the white snow. It was quite two miles away from the aeroplane itself, as the doctor had said.

'What a blessing it *did* fall off,' Aunt said.

'Yes, it fell off taking the fire with it. If it hadn't –' The man stopped speaking, took hold of his pony's bridle again and set off down the hill.

The white expanse of the valley between us and Angus's house and the white slopes of the Ben were all dotted with men and dogs moving about in long chains and I suddenly remembered why they were there and what they were doing. They were looking in all that wide place for one small baby. After that, I walked on beside Aunt without speaking but every time we passed a hummock of snow that was a bush underneath I walked round the back of it, hoping and hoping.

Soon we were in the clump of trees round the old church and I looked at the old broken building and thought of all the people who had gone to church there long ago and then we were out of the shadow of the trees, so that I saw Ben Vannich again and I thought how, at one time, it must have seen the church being built, must have heard the bell ring from the broken belfry, must have seen the people come out from their homes all over this valley and walk to church across the fields in summer and over the snow in winter. Ben Vannich, I thought, must have seen a great deal and must know a great deal but it did not tell what it knew. It kept everything secret, just as it was hiding the secret of the baby now and watching us all while we searched, saying nothing.

When we were near the bridge, three of the ponies stopped and one of the men said to Aunt: 'You will manage all right?'

'Of course we will!' Aunt told him. 'The children and I will manage perfectly. The rest of you go on up the Ben.'

'I will put a shot into the air in case some of them in the Glen have not seen us,' the man said and, loading his gun, he fired, making a great bang that echoed back from the Ben.

We three and Aunt started getting the buckets of soup, the bread and the bowls out of the baskets and soon the men gathered round us from all over the valley. It should have been a splendid picnic, I thought, with the soup steaming in the cold sunlight and the snow sparkling all round about but nobody spoke except to murmur, 'Thank you', to Aunt or us and there was no sound except the thud-thud of a heavy hammer from where some men and some policemen were making a fence of wire-netting round the aeroplane wing to keep the sheep away from it. Down below the bridge, the mother swan sat on her nest and the father swan swam up and down, whiter than the snow that lay on either side of the black water.

When all the men had been fed, we helped Aunt to pack the things into the baskets and Donald said: 'Do we have to go home now, Aunt?'

'Are you tired, Donald?' she asked.

'No!' he said. '*We* don't want to go home. Do we, Neil? Do we, Shona?'

'No!' we said.

'I'm not going yet anyhow,' Aunt said. 'I want to wait until the men come down from the Ben with the ponies. There might be – some news.'

Her face looked all sort of crumpled and I made a secret sign we have to Neil and Donald to go away so they took some left-over scraps of bread and went to feed the swans.

'Aunt,' I said, 'Neil, Donald and I – we know about – the baby.'

'Oh,' she said, looking down at me.

'Aunt, isn't there *anything* we can do?' I asked.

She shook her head, took out her handkerchief and looked away from me up towards Ben Vannich.

'Aunt,' I said, 'please don't cry,' but I knew she could not help it. 'Aunt, how old is the baby?'

'He is a little boy of seven months,' she said quietly. 'Now, Shona, run away and look after Neil and Donald. Don't go near the wreckage of the aeroplane and don't go too far. You ought not to be out here at all but I simply had to come.'

'We can go as far as the old church?' I asked.

'Yes. Yes. That will be all right,' she told me.

When I said to Neil and Donald that I thought we should leave Aunt alone for a while, Neil said: 'I am going to search.'

'Me too!' Donald said.

'*We* can't go up the Ben,' I told them.

'Not the Ben!' Neil said. 'I'm going over there!' He pointed to the side of the hill beyond the church where the main part of the aeroplane was lying. 'Nobody else is searching over there.'

'It's between the Ben and the church that they found all the people,' I said, 'and Aunt said not near the aeroplane.'

'Well, I'm going over there!'

'You are *not*, Neil Cameron!' I said. 'Aunt said not to go near the aeroplane. You don't care about anything except that aeroplane! You don't care about the baby or Aunt or anything! You're horrible!'

'I am not and I *do* care! You just want to boss everybody all the time and go where *you* want!'

'I do *not*!'

'You do!'

I swung my arm and hit Neil and then he rushed at me and we fell down in the snow.

'Shona! Neil!' Aunt's voice said very sternly. 'That is no way to behave! How dare you?'

We sat there in the snow, looking at her and feeling disgraced and terribly ashamed until Donald bent down and took one of my hands and one of Neil's saying: 'Come, Shona, get up. Come, Neil,' and we got to our feet.

'I am very sorry, Aunt,' I said.

'Me too,' said Neil.

She smiled at us a little bit. 'I know it's very difficult to behave oneself today,' she said, 'but do try. You may go up and look at the aeroplane if you like but don't go inside the wire-netting fence. And don't get in anybody's way.'

We set off over the valley and up the side of the hill to where the aeroplane was lying but on the way we looked in the hollows and among all the bushes but we could tell from all the footprints and marks where the snowdrifts had been dug over that all this place had been searched already. Somehow, we began to go more and more slowly up the hill, partly because the snow was getting deeper up here but partly because we did not care any more whether we got up to the place where the aeroplane was or not.

'I'm not going any further up there!' Neil said suddenly.

'Nor me either,' said Donald.

'I'm going somewhere where there are no footmarks!'

'Me too!' said Donald.

Instead of keeping on up the hill, we began to walk southward along the side of it and soon we came down into a little valley behind the old church but this place was full of footprints too.

'Shona,' Donald said, 'can you see owls in the day-time? I've never seen an owl.'

'I'm not sure,' I said. 'Do you know, Neil?'

Never before would I have asked Neil if he knew something that I did not know but today I did not care because I was thinking too much about the baby.

'You must be able to,' Neil said. 'They can't get invisible. Don't they sleep in the daytime in some sort of hidey-hole?'

'Yes,' Donald said. 'In the holes in trees and old buildings and places and they cough up all the skins and bones of the mice they have been eating and make owl pellets.'

'Owl pellets?' I said.

'Pellets yourself!' Neil said to Donald. '*Pellets!* You've got it all wrong! Spell it!'

'Pellets!' Donald shouted. 'Not spell-its!'

'I meant spell the *word*!' Neil said angrily.

'P-E-L-L-E-T-S – pellets!' Donald shouted. 'And they *do* cough them up and I haven't got it wrong! It's in the *Children's Encyclopedia* at home!'

'Is not!' Neil shouted.

'Is!' Donald yelled.

They were about to fly at one another just as Neil and I had done a little time ago when I put myself in between them. I could understand now that what was making us quarrel like this about things we did not care about in the least was that we could do nothing about the thing we cared about so much, which was the baby that was lost in the snow.

'I tell you what,' I said, 'let's go to the church and see if we can see the owl anyway. And if they do make these things out of mouseskins and cough them up they'll be dirty and grey and we'll find them easily in the snow.'

We went over to the old church. The whole end wall on this side was nearly broken down, probably because of the east wind striking it, and we went right inside among all the tangle of snowy, thorny bushes but we did not see the owl, although we went right to the other end and looked up into the ruined belfry. And we did not see anything that looked like coughed-up skins of mice either.

'That was a great big fib about those pellets, Donald Cameron!' Neil said.

'Was not!'

'It was! Just you wait till I get home and if –'

'Was *not* a fib!' Donald yelled.

It was then that I heard the owl give a little hoot.

'S-sh!' I said. 'Listen! The owl's there! We've woken it up.'

'Oo-oo!' the little noise came again and the boys

heard it too. It came from somewhere up in the ruined belfry, it seemed.

'Let's go outside,' Neil whispered. 'It must be outside among the ivy.'

We went as quietly as we could back through the tangle of bushes, out through the end wall again and came round to the outside of the belfry end but we could see nothing. Of course, the light was not good in there among the trees and there were a lot of holes in the belfry tower where loose stones had fallen out and all that ivy was hanging over it.

'Look here,' I said, 'we'd better get back a bit. That tower looks dangerous to me,' and I pulled Neil by the sleeve of his coat.

'Let go of me!' he said angrily and shook me off so that I fell on my back on the ground. I wanted to cry, lying there on the snow, because everything was so horrible but I stared hard upwards at the little bits of sky between the bare black branches of the trees that were just like thick lace, and blinked the tears out of my eyes.

And then I lay there and stared and stared, afraid to say a word. Away up there, lying among the intertwined branches of the trees, near an old bedraggled crow's nest, there was a pale blue carrying cot like the one our little brother Iain had when he was smaller. I simply lay there and stared at it. I could not say a word and when I tried to speak I began to cry instead.

'Shona,' Neil said, kneeling beside me, 'Are you hurt? I'm sorry.'

'Oh, *Shona*,' Donald said in the worried way he can say my name.

'No!' I managed to say. 'No, it's all right,' and then, as Neil pulled me up till I was sitting, I said: 'Neil! Donald! Look! Look up there! It's the *baby*!'

Everything was suddenly very quiet as we all looked up until there came again that sleepy little noise which we had thought was the owl.

'Ooo-oo!' said the baby. 'Ooo-oo!'

'Neil!' I said. 'You are the best runner! Run to Aunt! Quick!'

Neil went off like a shot out of Angus's gun. 'Tell her to bring somebody who can climb high trees!' I shouted after him but I do not think he heard.

'Shona,' Donald said as we both sat in the snow looking up at the blue cot, 'it's like "Rock-a-bye, baby, on the tree-top"!'

'Yes, Donald,' I said and I was glad that there had been no wind all day and that the cradle did not rock. I was crying again too but at the same time I thought that I had never been happier in my whole life.

7 We make some special arrangements

Suddenly the whole valley was full of bangs as shots were fired to tell everybody that the baby had been found and we saw all the people come running towards the old church.

It was Kenny who climbed to the very top of the tree, with several other men on branches lower down, and we all held our breath, watching, as he unhooked the handles of the cot from the branches and began to come down, cutting off a little branch here and there with his big knife to let the cot come through. Then it was handed down from one man to another until the last man took it in his hands above his head and brought it down to Aunt who was sitting on the ground and put it in her lap.

The baby was just as its mother must have put it to bed, strapped into its harness and dressed in a zipped-up suit that had gloves and feet on it and showed nothing but its face. He had been kicking and had got his blankets in a bit of a tangle and he began to kick again now. Aunt, with tears in her eyes but smiling all the same, looked up and around at everybody after a moment and said: 'This fellow is fine! He's just hungry. Where is that thermos of warm milk? Where's the sugar? Shona, take that cup and spoon from Kenny –'

The baby seemed to hear the spoon chinking on the cup as I stirred the sugar into the milk or maybe it was because he saw all the strange people around him but he suddenly began to cry very loudly and the queer thing was that all that crowd of men who had been so quiet until now suddenly began to laugh. I laughed too and so did the boys and while Aunt fed the baby he would bellow for the next spoonful and everybody would start laughing all over again. When the half-cupful of milk was finished, Aunt said: 'No, you are not going to have any more just now!' and then there was a proper row. The baby began to bellow in real earnest and his cries echoed all round the belfry of the old church and all round the trees so that Aunt and Kenny were almost shouting to make themselves heard when Kenny said: 'Oh, give him some more milk, poor fellow!'

'No, I *won't* give him any more, Kenny!' Aunt said. 'Let's get him home so that the doctor can see him first.'

Kenny almost snatched the cot from Aunt's knee and began to walk with long strides through the trees towards the track across the valley and the men all stood back, making a way for him and as he passed they all took their hats and caps off as if the baby was a king going by.

Then Aunt said: 'Shona and Neil, you two are quicker than any hill ponies. Run for home and tell the doctor that we've got the baby and that he's all right!'

Neil and I ran like anything across the valley and up the hill, not even feeling that we needed to stop for breath, and then on down the other side, through the back garden and into the house.

'Aunt said –' I panted, '– we've got the baby –' Neil panted, '– and he's all right!'

Angus and the doctor who had been sitting at the fire sprang up and stared at us.

'It was in a tree –'

' –at the old church!'

'God has mercy,' Angus said.

The doctor looked down at us very solemnly. 'This is really true?' he asked.

Neil and I looked at one another and then we looked at the doctor. 'As one Cameron to another,' we said.

Then he smiled at us and went to the telephone. 'Dr. Renfrew, please,' he said.

I think that was the best moment of all. I had not thought until then about how anxious the baby's mother and father must be, lying up there in hospital.

We had a lovely party when the baby came. The doctor took him out of his cot and he and Aunt took off his clothes and his dirty napkin and then the doctor examined him.

'He's in fine shape,' he said. 'His face is a little burned with the weather but that's all.'

'Shall I sponge him first or feed him, Doctor?' Aunt asked.

'For pity's sake,' Kenny said, 'give the poor fellow something to eat! I could eat a horse myself and I had two bowls of soup not two hours ago!'

The doctor laughed. 'Feed him first, Miss Cameron,' he said. 'And maybe Neil will run over the hill and bring back a pony or two for Kenny's supper.'

While Aunt fed the baby with more warm milk and bits of bread and butter, the rest of us had tea and bully beef sandwiches which we three made and then while Aunt sponged the baby he became very cheerful and started to pull Angus's beard but the doctor, as soon as Aunt had dressed the baby, fetched his coat from the hall and said: 'To the hospital, now, Miss Cameron, if you don't mind. I'll drive your car and you'll nurse the baby.'

'Yes,' Aunt said, talking to the baby and tickling him under his fat chin, 'we've only had a short loan of you, after all.'

While they were preparing to go, Neil made a secret sign to Donald and me and we followed him out to the hall. 'We've got to give the baby his hopes!' he whispered.

We had forgotten about the hopes until now and

we all stood looking at one another. It was not that we minded giving the baby the things that we had hoped for him but with Aunt and the doctor and Kenny and Angus there, we would have to explain about them and that was going to be very difficult.

'We'll never get them into his cot without being seen. Aunt doesn't take her eyes off that baby for a second,' I said and we all stood looking at one another for a little time more.

'We've got to manage somehow!' Neil said. 'It's all wrong if we don't and it has to be secret.'

I felt too that we must somehow give the things to the baby and in secret for, if we did not, we would spoil the hope in some horrible way.

'Angus knows about hopes,' Donald said.

'I bet Angus can keep secrets!' I said.

'Yes! Angus will help us,' Neil said and went back to the living-room while Donald and I stood in the doorway. 'Angus, will you come upstairs to our room for a moment, please?' he asked.

'What? Oh, yes, surely,' Angus said and got up at once.

'Please, Aunt, don't go away until we come down,' I said. 'We won't be a moment.'

In the boys' room, the three hopes were still lying on the chest of drawers on top of the flags and Neil said: 'Shona, you are the oldest. You explain to Angus.'

When there is anything difficult to be done in our family, Neil always remembers that I am the oldest.

'Angus,' I said, 'you remember you hoped a grave for that lamb-killing dog?'

'That is so,' Angus agreed gravely.

'Well – well, today when the baby was lost, Neil and Donald and I hoped these three things for him to have when he was found. We hoped these because they are our most favourite things. They are the things you gave us. We want the baby to have them now.'

'I see,' Angus said.

'People have to have their hopes, don't they, Angus?' Donald asked.

'To make it right, they have to, don't they?' Neil asked too.

'Yes. People have to have their hopes,' Angus agreed. 'To be right, people have to have their hopes.'

'So will you help us to give them to the baby all in secret?' I asked.

'Because they have to be secret,' Neil said.

'Yes, they are better, things like hopes, if they are secret,' Angus agreed again and he picked up the three things and put them into the pocket of his old tweed coat. 'We will just go down below,' he said, 'and see to it right away.'

When we were back in the living-room Angus did something that Neil and Donald and I could never have done but it was not only because he was old and grown-up that he could do it. It was because of that half-magic, secret power that he has sometimes. He went over to the sofa where the baby was falling asleep in his cot and stood up very straight and he made me think of Ben Vannich, as if he were far, far away from all of us and full of secrets and this half-magic power.

'Will you three people kindly turn your backs for a moment?' he said to Aunt, the doctor and Kenny. 'Shona and Neil and Donald and I have a little private business with this baby.'

Aunt glanced at us, then at Angus and at once turned her back without asking a single question and so did the doctor and Kenny. Angus took our hopes from his pocket, held them out to us and we took them. Then, very gently, he turned up the end of the little mattress that was under the baby's feet and we put the things in. He put the mattress back in place and then said to the baby: 'If life is not lucky for you, lad, it is not for want of hoping – All right, you can all turn round now,' he said to the others. Then he sat down in his chair again and began to poke the fire. Not one of them asked what we had done and I felt that, if they had, it would have been like asking a question of Ben Vannich. No answer would have come back.

Kenny picked up the cot with the baby in it.

'Keep the fire going until I get back, Shona,' Aunt said to me. 'And put all those sausages in the oven at Mark 3. And you boys peel enough potatoes to fill the big pan. Kenny and Angus must have a meal before they go back up the hill.'

'Not for me, thank you, Miss Cameron,' Kenny said. 'Much as I would like a few dozen sausages, I have to go back up right away to feed the ewes and lambs.'

'And I will just go up with Kenny,' Angus said.

'You will do nothing of the kind, Angus,' the doctor told him. 'You have walked quite enough on that ankle for one day. You will wait here until I get back from the hospital and come home with me for the night. Miss Cameron will lend me her car and we'll go round by the road to Vannich Village.'

'You could both stay here for the night,' Aunt said.

'No, thank you, I can't do that,' the doctor told her. 'Mrs. Greig's baby will be here before tomorrow and I must get back for that.'

'When do you sleep?' Aunt asked him.

'Every time I get the chance,' he said. 'You will wait here, Angus?'

'Oh, please stay, Angus!' we said.

'I will do just that,' Angus said. 'It is many years since I have had a day's outing like this. I went to the hospital in the doctor's car, of course, and stayed there for a week, but you could not call that an outing. It was not what you would truly call an outing.'

After the car had driven away, I put a lot of wood and coal on the fire and we all sat down on our stools round Angus's feet but before we could ask him about India or Egypt or the Argentine or anything, he said: 'I see you have two fine flags in the bedroom up yonder.'

Neil's face got all red in the firelight.

'What were you hoping to do with them?'

Neil took a deep breath. 'It was a silly idea I had when we left home to come here for the holidays, Angus,' he said, 'but I've given it up now. At least, I've not given it up exactly but I've changed it a bit.'

'What was the idea in the first of it, before you changed it?'

Neil's face was so red and he had got his fingers twisted into such a tangle that I simply had to help him a little.

'Angus, did you see Mount Everest when you were in India?' I asked.

'Yes, I did that,' he said. 'Now, yonder is a *proper* hill. Beside yon hill Ben Vannich up there is no better than a pimple.'

Angus calling Ben Vannich a pimple made us all giggle but in a secret, turning-our-faces-aside sort of way, as if we were afraid that the Ben would hear us and be insulted or angry.

'Did you try to climb Mount Everest when you were in India, Angus?' Donald asked.

'No, that I did not, Donald,' he said. 'Mount Everest is an Indian hill and I do not know about Indian hills. I only know a little about Highland ones and with hills it is better to stick to the ones you know.'

'You could have got a Sherpa to help you, maybe,' I said, 'like Sherpa Tensing helping Sir Edmund Hillary.'

'Ah, but Sir Edmund knew a good bit about Mount Everest himself,' Angus assured us. 'He must have been studying it for a long, long time. It was a great thing that they did, carrying their flags right to the top. I read all about it in a book from the library.'

'Father has that book at home,' I told him.

'Yes, it was a fine thing that they did and grand to

read about. Old as I am now, it made me want to go out and climb Ben Vannich and put my Seaforth pipe-banner on the top of it!'

'That's what I wanted to do, Angus,' Neil said all in a rush. 'The flags upstairs, I brought them to put on top of Ben Vannich!'

Angus smiled, not in a nasty way, but very softly and gently. 'You are a little short in the leg for Ben Vannich, yet, lad,' he said, 'but you will grow. Yes, you will grow. You come of Vannich people. Your grandfather was a big man and your great-grandfather was a big, long wiry man like Kenny. These are the kind of men that climb Ben Vannich – men that carry no weight except the weight of their bones and their muscles and their brains – So what were you planning for the flags since you cannot get them to the top of Ben Vannich as yet?'

'I'm going to put them on the Cairn on Jenny Hill,' Neil said sadly. 'After all, that's the highest I've been.'

'You are not quite right there, I am thinking.'

'How do you mean, Angus?'

'You have been a lot higher than that. You have been up to my house. That is a lot higher than Jenny Hill.'

'Is it?'

At first, I was as surprised as Neil was about this and I looked into the fire and thought about our walk up to Angus's. Looking at the burning heap of coal and wood was a little like looking at a range of red and black mountains and I remembered that we made the long steep climb up Jenny Hill, and then, although we went down the slope to the valley where the church was, we had not gone down anything like as steeply as we had come up. Then, after we had crossed the bridge, we had begun to climb again along the winding path where the river flowed past us so fast that there were stony cataracts and even little waterfalls in some places. Even when we reached Angus's garden gate, I remembered, the path sloped steeply upwards to the door of his house.

'Of course it is!' I said to Neil when all this had flashed through my mind. Angus's house is twice as high as Jenny Hill.'

'Oh, rot!' Neil said.

'No, Neil,' Angus told him. 'Your sister is right. Jenny Hill is a little over five hundred feet above sea level but my house is eleven hundred and seventy feet up.'

'Golly!' Neil said. 'That means I've been nearly a third of the way up Ben Vannich!'

'It does indeed. And if I were you, do you know what I would do?'

'What Angus?'

'I would bring your flags to my house the first fine day and we will plant them there, on the highest bit at the side of the house. When I was in the Seaforths, we always had a flag flying at our barracks and I do not see why I should not have a flag flying at my house. And besides, there is another thing that I am thinking. If I had a flag pole, I would get another big red flag or maybe a pure white one and fly it when I wanted Kenny or Roddy to come in for something special. It would save me firing my gun and wasting cartridges when they are such a terrible price.'

As a rule, when Aunt has to go away and leave us alone in the house – she does not do it very often – it is always very tedious. It is not so bad if the day is fine and we can go out but even then we do not like it very much. On this day, it would have been very tedious because our legs were too tired to go out any more – especially Donald's – but Angus being there with us made it quite different. By the time he had told us how he would get his Forestry Commission friends to give him the trunk of a young larch tree for a flag-pole and we had made one or two other plans, we heard the car stop outside and Aunt and the doctor were back.

'Well,' she said, 'what a splendid fire! And what have you been doing all this long time?'

'We have just been making a few certain special arrangements which you will be hearing about in due course,' Angus told her. 'And now the doctor and I must be going.' He picked up his tweed hat and took his tall crook from the corner where it stood. Then he looked round at us three. 'On Monday morning,' he told us, 'Kenny and I will see to the erecting of the pole and on the first fine day after that, we will be expecting you all at Croft o' Vannich. Thank you for a fine *ceilidh* and goodnight to you all,' and he went away out to the car.

'What pole was Angus talking about?' Aunt asked.

'Not telling!' Neil said quickly. 'It's to be a surprise.'

'Aunt, what's a kaylay like Angus said?' Donald asked.

'*Ceilidh* is the Gaelic word for an entertainment round the hearth or even just a pleasant chat by the fire. That's what he meant when he thanked you people. What did you talk about?'

'Not telling!' Neil said again. 'It was a few certain special arrangements which you will be hearing about in due course.'

'Aunt,' I said, 'tell about the baby! Were his father and mother pleased?'

'Yes, Shona, they were very, very pleased.'

She had taken off her mackintosh and she sat down at the fire with it in a bundle on her lap.

'They are going to write to you three later on,' she said. 'But will you tell me something? Was it you three and Angus who put those cartridge cases and the sprig of white heather in the baby's cot?'

'Yes, Aunt,' I said and all three of us looked down at the floor.

'The baby's mother was terribly pleased when she found them. I told her I thought you had put them there. She said she will keep them always. But why did you do it?'

'They were hopes,' I said.

'Hopes?'

'Yes, just hopes,' Neil said.

'Yes, three hopes, Aunt,' Donald said.

'I see,' said Aunt but, of course, she did not really see. What she meant was that she saw it was a secret and that she would not ask us any more about it.

'Shona,' she said, 'hang up my coat for me and I'll go and hope up some supper.'

8 Hope-magic under Ben Vannich

THE next day was Sunday and, when we got up in the morning, all the snow and frost had gone and it was pouring with rain. It went on pouring all day Monday and Tuesday and Wednesday and we had to go home on the Saturday so we began to think that we would never get up to Angus's at all.

'It's not the rain I mind,' Aunt said. 'After all, we're not made of sugar and we won't melt but we'd never find our way in all that cloud above Jenny Hill.'

'There's the sheep-track, Aunt,' Neil said. 'All we have to do is follow it.'

'Up there, Neil, there is a perfect network of sheep-tracks and it is too easy to get off one and on to another and wander round in circles for hours.'

'We could take a great big ball of string and un-wind it behind us,' Donald suggested.

But, of course, we all knew that it was no use making suggestions and that Aunt would not set out for Angus's until the weather cleared.

'We could try a bit of hope on these flags again,' I said early on the Thursday morning when we were all in the boys' room. 'After all, it worked the last time.'

Neil stared out at the rain. 'I don't think you can hope the same thing twice,' he said. 'Once you've hoped it, it's hoped for good. That hope we did on those flags turned out far better than we ever hoped anyway.'

'Yes,' Donald said, 'we only hoped them for a fine day to put them on Jenny Hill and they've gone and got hoped away up to Angus's.'

'The point is that they haven't!' I said. 'They can't get there because of the rain!'

'Look here,' Neil said, 'we've never really *hoped* them to Angus's. We just *decided* we would plant them up there and that is quite a different thing!'

He sprang out of bed and Donald and I sprang out of Donald's. Neil fetched his haversack from the cupboard and we put in it the flags and a box of sweets we had bought for Angus, fastened it and put it on the chest of drawers.

'Listen!' I said before we did any more, 'I heard Aunt's bed creak. We've never once made early tea for her this holidays and I've got an idea that these hopes work better if you are not just thinking about what you yourself want to do all the time. You've got to put something into hopes, something practical, like

Aunt said, like Angus getting his spade and digging a grave for that lamb-killer.'

'All right,' Neil said. 'Let's go and make some tea for Aunt. I don't see how it can do much good but it can't do any harm. Come on, Donald!'

'No. I've got something to do here, another hope thing,' Donald told us.

'Oh, all right,' Neil said. 'But don't you touch that haversack, mind!'

Neil and I went down to the kitchen and made tea and toast for Aunt and carried it up to her room. Aunt's bedroom has two windows, one that looks out over the Firth and one in the gable that looks towards Jennyville and when she sat up in bed the first thing she did was to look out of this west window.

'It's still raining,' I said, 'so you needn't bother looking.'

'So it is! What a shame! But what a lovely tray. It *was* kind of you to bring it,' she said and I was ashamed because we had forgotten every morning until now how much she likes to have early tea brought to her.

'After this,' she said, pouring out a cup, 'if I don't think of something interesting for us to do today, I'm a Dutchman!'

We left her with the tea and went back to the boys' room. Donald was standing beside the chest of drawers where the haversack was lying but alongside it now there were three rather nasty-looking grey furry round things about the size of biggish marbles.

'What are these?' I asked.

'Owl pellets,' he said.

'What?' Neil picked one up, peered closely at it, smelled it and put it down again. 'Where did you get them?'

'From Kenny. He found them in the tree where the baby was.'

'And you never told us! Donald Cameron, you are a mean, sneaky little beast!'

'Am *not*!' Donald said. 'You didn't believe in owl pellets when I told you about them, Neil Cameron, so why should I go telling?'

'Donald is quite right, Neil,' I said. 'You were horrid about owl pellets that day at the church. And besides, *they're* horrid too, nasty vomited-up mouse skins that they are!'

'Don't you like them, Shona?' Donald asked, hurt. 'Don't you think they are interesting?' He blinked at me through his glasses. 'I bet nobody in my class at school has ever seen an owl pellet.'

I am in the Second Form at High School and I suddenly thought that probably none of my friends had ever seen an owl pellet either.

'Oh, yes, Donald,' I said. 'They are awfully interesting and not so horrid when you get used to them a bit.'

'Then that's all right because I was going to hope one to you and one to Neil for a fine day for going to Angus's.'

'Oh, Donald!' I said.

'Oh, gosh!' Neil said.

'But Shona has to have first pick, Neil,' said Donald.

'I don't mind. They are all about the same size anyway.'

'I choose that one,' I said, pointing. It did not look quite so mousy and nasty as the other two.

'I choose that one,' Neil said.

'All right.' Donald put his right hand over the one I had chosen. 'I hope this owl pellet to Shona for a fine day to go to Angus's,' he said and then he moved his hand to Neil's, 'and I hope this one to Neil for a fine day to plant his flags at Angus's – You can take them now,' he told us, 'but you have to be careful with them or they'll all crumble up. You'd better put them in your sweet boxes. That's where *I* keep them.'

I took my pellet to my room and put it on the very corner of the dressing-table and was on my way back to the boys to hope the haversack when I heard Aunt calling me.

'Shona,' she said when I went into her room, 'it's going to clear! Look at that rainbow to the west there. You and the boys get dressed and we'll have breakfast and set off to Angus's. It will be very wet underfoot so put on Wellington boots and put your slippers in your haversacks!'

I ran back to the boys.

'Hurry up, you!' Neil said. 'We've got to hope this haversack!'

'We don't have to!' I said. 'Donald's owl pellets did it! Aunt says to get ready to go to Angus's'

While we had breakfast and washed up and packed our contribution to the lunch, the rain stopped, the sun came out and everything was all sparkly with rain-drops, but the clouds were still hiding Ben Vannich. As Aunt had said it was very splashy and wet under-foot, especially on the other side of the hill, going down to the old church where we stopped for our first rest.

When I first saw that church, it seemed to me to be a terribly sad place but it did not feel like that any more because, now, it was connected up in my mind with that splendid moment when I saw the baby's cot away up in the branches.

'I see a thing!' Neil said suddenly as we went to-wards the fallen stones by the wall to sit down.

When we all looked, it was a primrose, looking out from among its green leaves by the side of a stone.

'I feel like giving Neil full marks for that,' Aunt said, 'because it means that Spring is really here at last.'

When we reached the little bridge, it was quite exciting, for the water which had been away down below us the last day we were here was now actually flowing over the path across the bridge and we had to paddle through it.

'It's the rain,' Aunt said, 'and the snow has been melting on the Ben. Look!'

When we looked up at Ben Vannich, the clouds had rolled themselves away up into the sky and the Ben was no longer white all over as it had been a few days ago. The lower parts of it were grey and brown and pale green now but its top was still white, as if it were wearing a hat.

'These swans are going to be in trouble,' Aunt said

next and, at first, I did not know what she meant but then I saw that, on the lower side of the bridge where the nest was, the river was spreading away out over the swamp-land, three or four times as broad as it had been when we last saw it.

'What will happen to them?' I asked.

'If the river gets much bigger, their nest will be washed away.'

The big father swan seemed to think this too, for he was not swimming about and hissing, with his wings all curved up, or being the Lord High Cockalorum of the river any more. He was standing beside the nest on his big, awkward, flat black feet, watching the rushing, spreading water, and looking silly, bedraggled and pathetic.

'What a shame!' I said.

'Yes, but maybe the river is at its worst now,' Aunt said. 'It never usually gets as high as this even. Maybe the nest will escape after all.'

Anyhow, as Aunt said, there was nothing we could do to help the swan for wild creatures are very difficult to help because they are so afraid of people, so we left him standing there beside his wife on the nest and went on by the river to Angus's.

When we reached the house, Angus and Kenny were at the garden gate and Angus said: 'Yes, we have been watching you through the glasses since you came over Jenny Hill. I am getting a real smell of Spring in the air today and I was thinking you would come. But come over to the wall here for I have something to show you.'

At the wall, Kenny lifted the three of us on to the top and Angus said: 'Now, you see where the snow stops yonder on the side of the Ben? You see that big rock shaped like Kenny's nose?'

We said we recognized the rock he meant.

'Well, Shona,' he said, 'take these glasses of mine –' he handed up to me his heavy field glasses – 'and set them to suit your eyes on that rock.'

I twiddled the little wheel on the glasses and the rock became bigger and bigger and clearer and clearer. 'I can see a little bush growing out of the side of the rock, Angus,' I said.

'All right. Now bring your glasses down to the bottom of that rock and see what you see.'

'Another bush,' I said, 'and oh, a waterfall – and – oh gosh!'

'What, Shona? What? What?' the boys were asking.

'Don't tell!' Kenny said.

So I did not say what I saw but at the bottom of that rock, which was really a cliff, there were seven deer grazing and one of them was simply enormous. While I watched, it raised its head and seemed to look straight at me so that I felt as if it saw me. I could have watched it for ages but, of course, the boys were clamouring now to have a look.

When everybody had had a turn of the field glasses, Angus said: 'It is not many people that get a sight of old Vannich.'

'Vannich?' Aunt asked.

'Yes. We call that old stag Vannich. It is a pity that

it is so early in the year and he has not his antlers as yet. He is a royal stag with as fine a head as there is in these hills in the season.'

'But where are his antlers now, Angus?' I asked.

'He sheds them every year, Shona,' Angus told me, 'and grows himself a new set every spring. By the month of August, he will have a big spread of twelve points or more.'

'Cows don't get new horns every year,' Neil said.

'No, but deer do,' Angus told us. 'And a queer thing is that the horns of cows are hollow but the antlers of deer are solid. But they drop off the deer at the beginning of winter.'

'I wish we could see Vannich with his antlers on,' I said. 'Perhaps we *shall*, in the summer holidays, Angus?'

'I doubt it,' he said. 'I doubt if Vannich will come down within range of the glasses in the summer. He is by a long way the wisest and most cunning fellow in these parts, even counting the human fellows. Many a man has spent many a day trying to get within firing range of these antlers of his but none of them ever have. And Vannich knows who his friends are. He knows that Kenny or Roddy or I will not harm him, the old rascal – that is why he brought his ladies down there for a feed after the storm. You would never see him down there in the shooting season – Well, come away into the house now and have a rest after your walk.'

We three were looking for the flag-pole but although we looked all round we saw nothing and I began to wonder if Angus had forgotten, but I did not really think so. However, it was splendid to go into that lovely half-magic house again and see the big gypsy pot steaming above the fire and the Willow Pattern china on the shelves catching the light.

'You would see that the aeroplane was taken away as you came across the Glen?' Angus asked. 'Yes. They were very quick about it. Two days they were working at it when they had it all away.'

'How did they get it away?' Neil asked.

'They took most of it to pieces and loaded everything into tractor trailers,' Kenny told us.

Angus made a big jug of cocoa but instead of giving Kenny a cup like everybody else, he gave him another jug and said: 'You had better make a jugful for yourself, Kenny. You are a little like the well at Vannich Village for I do not think that your stomach has any bottom in it or top, either, come to that.'

'Did *you* see the men taking the aeroplane away, Angus?' Donald asked.

'Oh, yes. I went down to see them special. I went down to tell them that I was in need of a flag-pole.'

'Why, Angus?' Neil asked.

'Well, it struck me that a good long bit of that aeroplane would make a fine flag-pole and it would be metal that would not rot with the weather as a larch pole would do through time. And then, the men who were there were all engineers and mechanics and clever people like that, so they put little wheels on it for the ropes to go up and down. A very good job they made of it, did they not, Kenny?'

Kenny nodded his head.

'So,' said Angus, 'it is out there at the back of the house. We did not put it up as yet although we have dug the hole for it, for we thought you would all be giving us a hand and then we will ask your Auntie to run up the flags for the first time. I always think that things like raising flags and the launching of ships are better if done by a lady. If you are all finished eating for the present, especially Kenny, we will just go out there right away. The sooner we get that pole up, the sooner these flags will be flying.'

It was a beautiful flag-pole. It was nearly as long as Angus's house and bright silver and when we went out Kenny poured water on a heap of cement and sand he had lying on the ground and began to mix it with a shovel. When the cement was ready, Angus put four quite big stones in the deep hole and then the rest of us got in a line along the pole and lifted it while Angus guided the end of it into position among the stones at the bottom of the hole. Then he told Neil and Donald and me to hold it in position and he went tramping off across the garden, climbed the wall and went away up the Glen. When he was quite a long way off, he turned to face us and waved one arm up towards Ben Vannich.

'A little to the right,' Kenny said and pushed the pole. Angus waved again. 'No, too much,' Kenny said and we pushed it back a little and after some more pushing to and fro, Angus put both his arms straight up.

'Right, boys!' Kenny said then and Neil and Donald

and I began to slosh the cement into the hole while Kenny put some stones in now and then, and all the time Angus signalled back to us when the pole got out of its position.

When all the cement was in, Neil came running out with his flags but Kenny told us we would have to wait until just before we went home to run them up because the cement must get time to set.

'It will be quite hard by the early evening,' he said. 'It is the quick stuff. We got it special because this was an urgent job.'

'So the three of you will just have to be patient and wait,' Aunt said.

'Do you know the best way to be patient?' Kenny asked.

'No,' we told him.

'Do *not* be patient,' he said. 'Go and do something else and there is a thing or two we have to do anyway. I could do with a little more cocoa and then we must furl these flags so that they will break open in the proper way when we run them up later on.'

Kenny, we discovered, had been in the Navy during the war like Father and he knew all about flags and signals and everything, so while he and the boys fixed the flags – there were four altogether now for Angus had contributed a Union Jack and Kenny a St. Andrew's Cross – Aunt and I helped Angus to prepare the lunch.

'Angus,' Aunt said while we peeled the potatoes, 'do you think the river will rise much more? If it does, that swan's nest down at the bridge will be carried away.'

'I was just telling these swans that very thing only yesterday,' Angus said. 'And it is not the first year that I have told them, either, but they are so stupid and untellable a pair of birds as you would meet in a day's march. And there is nothing more certain than that the river is not nearly at its height yet. There is a lot of snow still to come down from the Ben and it is going to thaw fast and come down fast. However, as soon as we have had our dinner, we will go down there and shift that nest.'

Aunt dropped the potato she was peeling with a splash into the water.

'Shift it, Angus?'

'If it is not shifted, it will be washed away.'

'But how *can* you shift it? The cob swan will never let you near it!'

'Oh, yes, he will. He will hiss a little, likely, and that kind of nonsense but he will let me shift it all right. He always has before.'

'You've moved their nest before?'

'Oh, yes, a dozen times if not more. Every year, I am telling these swans to build further from the river but they will *not* do it so I just have to shift them.'

'And the pen swan goes back to the nest all right?' Aunt asked.

'Oh, yes. Indeed, she has a lot more sense than the cob. He is not good for anything but swimming up and down looking pleased with himself and being rude to people.'

'He wasn't looking pleased with himself today, Angus,' I said.

'No. It is quite likely that he is wondering in that foolish head of his that is too small to hold any brains if I have forgotten about him and his nest, but I have not forgotten. We will go down there after dinner. Maybe, Shona, you will scrub the earth off this lot of potatoes and put them and all the peelings into this pan and we will boil them for the swans. They are quite fond of a boiled potato.'

As soon as we had finished dinner and had done the washing-up, we all set off down to the bridge, we three riding ponies with bundles of branches tied on in front of us, Angus and Kenny carrying spades and Aunt with the boiled potatoes and peelings in a bucket. The river was absolutely rushing down the Glen now, making a roaring noise, and when we came to the bridge, Angus said: 'Kenny, you are going to have to carry Shona and her brothers over the bridge when they go home.'

The flood water was now even nearer to the swan's nest than it had been when we passed earlier and the father swan was walking round and round the nest as if his brain were going round and round in circles with not knowing what to do.

'You people wait here,' Angus said at the edge of the swamp. 'Just give me those potatoes and I will go and have a word or two with that foolish creature.'

With his spade over his shoulder, the bucket of potatoes in his hand, Angus went sloshing across the swamp in his Wellington boots and the father swan

came to meet him, curved up his wings, pushed his neck out and began to hiss.

'Kenny,' Aunt said in a whisper, 'that great brute could easily knock Angus down!'

'Oh, he will not do that,' Kenny said. 'Just wait a little.'

Angus stopped in front of the swan. 'Now then,' he said sternly, 'what foolishness is this again this year? Have you no brains in that head of yours? Here, take a potato!' He threw two or three potatoes out of the bucket and the swan began to eat them as the mother swan rose carefully from her nest and began to walk towards Angus.

'So it is six eggs you have?' he said to her. 'A fine big family and what foolish sort of place is that to build your nest?' He threw a few more potatoes out of the bucket. 'If all swans were as stupid as you there would be no swans in the world at all – Come, Kenny!' he called then.

Kenny went over beside him and they began to dig up clods with their spades and pile them up in a heap so Aunt and the three of us crept in a little nearer to them.

Angus went on scolding the swans in a stern voice all the time he was digging and then he would give them another potato and go on scolding and digging again.

'What are they doing, Aunt?' Donald asked.

'Building a sort of island, I think,' Aunt said. 'You see, if they take the nest too far from where the swans built it, the mother swan might not go back to it.'

In a little while, Kenny came over and took the branches we had brought and Angus mixed them in with clods of earth, put more clods on top, then more branches and more clods until there was a little hill about as high as Donald and flat on top.

'Bring me one or two dry divots from over there, Kenny,' Angus said then.

When the dry, grassy clods had been laid on top of the hill, Angus threw a great lot of potatoes out of the bucket all round about, waited till the swans were eating them and threw aside his spade, but he did not stop talking in his scolding, grumbling voice.

'Six eggs you have,' he said, bending over the nest and getting his hands underneath all the sticks and rushes it was made of, 'and it would serve you right if Kenny took the whole lot home and ate them for his tea although goodness knows he would need a pound of ham along with them, likely. Never in my life have I seen a sillier pair of birds than you two!'

He was suddenly walking with the eggs in his hands as if they were on a tray made of twigs over to the little hill where he put the nest down very carefully and then he put the last of the potatoes from the bucket all round it. He then stopped scolding, came over to us and said: 'We'll go away a bit now and wait a little.'

By this time, the swans had eaten up all the scattered potatoes and peelings and the mother one went back to the place where her nest had been but, of course, it was not there. She began to walk about in circles and so did the father until they both discovered there were more potatoes on the little hill. They reached up with their long necks, pulled them down and ate them until there were no more in sight and then they began to scrabble up to the top looking for more. It was then that the mother swan discovered the eggs but she put her head on one side and looked at them, put her head the other way and looked at them again, poked in among them with her beak and walked all round them before she decided they were really hers. At last, she put her legs wide apart, sat down, arranged the eggs under her feathers with her beak and then looked round haughtily all about her as if she were a very snobbish queen sitting on a throne. The father swan walked once round the hill, then went over to the water and began to swim, his wings curved up in great pride, as if he himself had built that throne for his wife.

'Look at him, the poor conceited idiot!' Angus said and that described that bird exactly.

'Why did you scold them all the time, Angus?' I asked.

'Partly because I felt like scolding them because they are so foolish, Shona,' he told me, 'and partly because the only thing a human being can do better than any animal or bird can do is to speak words. You can do a lot with animals by speaking to them. It impresses them I am thinking – Well, we must go back up the hill. That cement should be fairly firm by now if what the mason said about it is true and Donald the mason is a fairly honest man – Dear me, Kenny! Look at where you have left your spade! You are nearly as foolish as that swan and no good for anything but eating potatoes. Never mind, I will get it.'

Angus went back over towards the swan's hill to where they had been working and picked up the spade but then he began to dig again down into the wet hole they had made. After a little, he came over to us carrying a great dollop of mud on the spade.

'There is something here that is not Glen Vannich mud,' he told us, 'and I am just inquisitive to see what it is – it is a bit of a dish. Sometimes I will be findng little bits of things that belonged to the old people of before the time of the Clearances.'

He pushed the mud off the spade with his boot and began to spread it out. We saw a curved piece of brownish earthenware like the bottom of a big vase. Angus turned it over with the spade and it was white on the other side and looked like a large chipped saucer full of mud. He picked it up, pulled up some grass and wiped it and suddenly something fell to the ground and clinked against the spade.

'Kenny!' Angus said. 'It is my granny's pudding-bowl! That is a half-sovereign!' Then he looked up at Ben Vannich. 'I trust that I am not a greedy man but there is no harm in hoping,' he said. 'I hope there are some more in it!'

I had meant to tell that, during the four rainy days down at the house, I had been thinking quite a lot about all the hoping we had done this holiday but I could not make up my mind about it. Sometimes I would decide that it was a childish game and that, although Neil and Donald believed in it, I was too old and grown-up now to take it seriously. When we had first hoped the flags for a fine day, I told myself, the kind of weather that it was gong to be had already been decided by the cyclones and anti-cyclones that the weather people are always talking about. When we hoped the things for the baby, I told myself, he would have been found within an hour of our seeing him in the tree by the helicopter that came up from the aerodrome that afternoon. And this very morning, when I had suggested hoping the flags again and had taken part in the hoping of the owl pellets, it was not because I really believed in it but because I thought it would cheer up the boys. But now, when Angus looked up at Ben Vannich and hoped his hope, I was believing in it with all my heart and when the others put their hands under the chipped piece of pottery, I put my hands under it too and I was hoping as hard as I could that Angus would find some more of his granny's half-sovereigns.

He wiped again with the grass.

'Here's one!' Kenny said.

'I've got one!' Donald shouted.

'Three of them.' Angus said quietly. 'That is just what I hoped. That is the best haul that anybody ever got out of the river, Kenny.'

He looked down at us. 'One for each of you,' he said.

'Oh, no, Angus!' Aunt said. 'You must keep them!'

'Oh, but *so*!' Angus told her. 'One each for Shona, Neil and Donald and I will keep the bottom of Granny's pudding-bowl!'

The three of us did not speak a word as the ponies plodded up the track to the house again, for finding real buried golden treasure like that is a thing for which there are no words. We simply sat on the ponies with our half-sovereigns clutched in our hands and it was not till we had run round to where the flag-pole was that we found words again. Neil bent down and poked the cement very gingerly with one finger.

'It's hard,' he said and then tapped it with the edge of his half-sovereign. 'Hard as a brick! Hurray! Hurray!'

Shouting, we all danced round the pole for a little while like wild Indians.

'Let's put our half-sovereigns lying on the cement round the pole,' I said then.

'What for?' Neil asked.

'They'll look pretty lying there.'

And they did look pretty, glinting in the sunshine.

'Look!' I said to Aunt when she and Angus and Kenny came round.

'Aren't they beautiful?' she said. 'Are you leaving them there for the ceremony?'

'Yes.'

'Tell me,' she said, 'are they hopes?'

'Yes, I think they are, sort of,' I answered.

'Before we put the flags up,' Angus said, 'we will have tea for if Kenny does not get a little to eat, the strength to blow will go out of him.'

So we all went into the house and had tea out of the Willow Pattern teapot and the Willow Pattern cups but Kenny had a Willow Pattern bowl of broth out of the gypsy pot as well.

'Angus,' Donald asked, 'what did you mean about Kenny having the strength to blow?'

'To blow the pipes, lad,' Angus said. 'I am a little old for the pipes myself now but I taught Kenny to play them and he is not bad at them at all, although it is myself that says so, and he will give us a tune when the flags go up.'

When we went outside, the sky was getting pink with evening.

'Red sky at night, shepherd's delight!' Donald said.

'And that is true, lad,' Angus said. 'And the red sky at morning is the shepherd's warning.'

The snow on Ben Vannich had turned pale pink too, which seemed to give it a more friendly look although it was still mysterious and had an air of half-magic and Angus suddenly became half-magic too as he stood looking away up to it.

'I am very fond of the Ben,' he said then, and we were all quiet for a moment.

Aunt held Kenny's pipes for him while he fixed the flags, which he had done up in little parcels, to the ropes of the pole, and then he gave the end of a rope to Aunt.

'Just give it a long, steady pull,' he said, 'and they should be all right,' and he took the pipes from her, put them on his shoulder and began to blow.

Our half-sovereigns glittered in the pink light, we all stood in a circle round the pole and when the pipes began to play Aunt pulled on the rope. The little flag

parcels went up and up and up and at last they all
broke free, fluttering in the breeze like four brightly-
coloured hopes and, away behind them, there was the
rose-coloured snow on the peak of Ben Vannich.

Some years ago, some young friends of mine complained that I kept on writing books for their mother and father to read and none for them, and that this was very unfair. I told them that if they would give me some idea of the kind of book they would like, I would try to write it. At this time, these young people were taken everywhere by car, and they wanted very much to make a journey by train, and Shona, the eldest said: 'It should be a story about a railway journey.' Neil, her biggest brother, said: 'It should be about us having a terrific adventure on a train, all by ourselves, without mother or father or anybody like that there.' Donald, the next brother, said: 'And we would pull the communication cord and stop the train, and the police would come and drag the criminals off to prison.' And Iain, the baby brother, merely said: 'Bang, bang!' because he was too young at the time to say much else.

That was how my first children's book came to be written. CAMERONS ON THE HILLS *was my second, and I was led to write it because of a piece in the newspaper about an aeroplane crash in the South of France in which several people were killed, and a baby was lost for several hours, and then discovered caught in a bush on the side of a cliff.*

JANE DUNCAN

Poyntzfield

Ross-shire

1967